Unified Field Theory

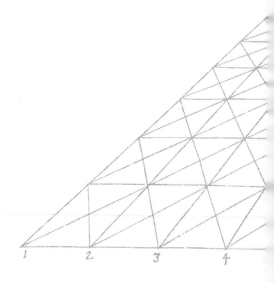

Unified Field Theory

STORIES BY FRANK SOOS

The University of Georgia Press | Athens and London

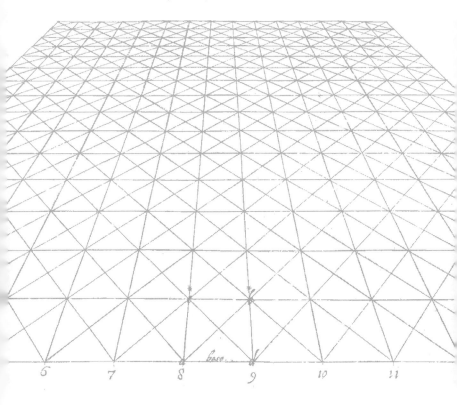

© 1998 by Frank Soos
Published by the University of Georgia Press
Athens, Georgia 30602
All rights reserved

Designed by Erin Kirk New
Set in 10 on 13 Ehrhardt by G&S Typesetters
Printed and bound by Maple-Vail

The paper in this book meets the guidelines for
permanence and durability of the Committee on
Production Guidelines for Book Longevity of the
Council on Library Resources.

Printed in the United States of America

02 01 00 99 98 C 5 4 3 2 1

Library of Congress Cataloging in Publication Data

Soos, Frank.
Unified field theory : stories / by Frank Soos.
p. cm.
"The Flannery O'Connor Award for short fiction."
ISBN 0-8203-2048-X (alk. paper)
I. Title.
PS3569.O663U55   1998
813′.54—dc21   98-14342

British Library Cataloging in Publication Data available

"Nickerson's Luck" first appeared in
the *Cimarron Review* and is reprinted with the
permission of the publisher.

For Susan, with love

Acknowledgments

The author would like to thank these literary magazines for publishing the following stories: "Nickerson's Luck," *Cimarron Review;* "When the Hoot Owl Moves Its Nest," *Timber Creek Review;* "If You Meet the Buddha by the Road," *Grain;* "Trip to Sometimes Island" as "Sometimes Island" in *Bellingham Review;* and "Key to the Kingdom," *O. Henry Festival Stories, 1991.*

Thanks to the National Endowment for the Arts and the Alaska State Council on the Arts for fellowships supporting the completion of these stories.

And thanks to the many friends who encouraged me in my work, especially to my wife, Susan Blalock, and to Kes Woodward and Janis Lull. Thanks to Charles East for his generous work as editor and to my friend Jennifer Brice, who was always ready to lend a hand with the copyediting.

Contents

Nickerson's Luck

1

When the Hoot Owl Moves Its Nest

24

If You Meet the Buddha by the Road

38

Trip to Sometimes Island

72

Ray's Boat

99

Key to the Kingdom

132

Unified Field Theory

148

Unified Field Theory

Nickerson's Luck

Because Nickerson hit a dog, he lost a hubcap. He discovered it missing days later, and, while he had no proof, felt its loss was a result of hitting the dog. The connection wasn't physical. He struck the dog with his front bumper and continued over it with the right front wheel, but it was the hubcap off the left rear wheel that was missing.

For days after his discovery Nickerson slowly patrolled his route to and from work looking for it among the tall weeds and litter. Which way had he been headed? At what speed? Where, he wondered, had he hit a hole deep enough to spring it free? Maybe it had been stolen; maybe it had been lost days before and he never noticed until that particular morning, the morning of the day he and his wife were to sign their separation agreement.

He showed her the exposed white wheel, the raw lug nuts, like the ugly naked foot of an old man, and she could see he was genuinely aggrieved. "Honey, it's gone, get yourself another one," she told him and touched him lightly on the shoulder. Francine still wished him only happiness. He wasn't ready for that yet.

His search for the hubcap was futile, but he refused to think in such terms. Instead he remembered the dogs, a pack of them, litter mates, coming up onto the highway. Maybe they imagined they were after a rabbit, maybe they were running for the stupid joy of it. Nickerson, driving his wife from a session with the marriage counselor, was relieved to see them. But then the dogs were swarming around his car, and then one was under his wheel. He felt the bump as he rolled over it, and when he looked in the mirror he could see it back in the road, twitching. Thinking he would have to kill it the rest of the way, he fished his tire iron out of the trunk and started back to it.

The other dogs gathered around it, drew up the new smell of death into their nostrils, and moved off across the road. By then it had quit moving. He examined it anyway just to make sure it was dead and pushed the carcass onto the shoulder with his foot. It had the soft fur of a pup. Then he looked around. There was a small wooden house, the only place around the dogs could belong to. He went up to the house and knocked.

Inside a television set had lost its hold on the vertical and was flipping its picture wildly. He could hear the sound through the door, but could see no people. The living room floor was scattered with stray articles of clothing: a child's sock, a brassiere, a gnawed-up shoe on a dark green rug. Glasses and cans sat on the arms of beat-up stuffed chairs. A gold vinyl couch had a powder blue blanket pushed down to one end, as if somebody had just been lying there trying to watch the broken TV. He looked beyond to where the room opened into the kitchen stacked with dirty plates, pots and pans, boxes of cereal, a spilled bag of dog food on the floor. But no matter how hard he knocked on the door or pecked on the windowpane, nobody came to answer. He went back to comfort his crying wife. It had been a hard session.

None of the sessions had done any good. Nickerson had come to see their marriage as luckless. First they tried not to have children, but some ingenious sperm sneaked through. It found an egg, and they got together. But Nickerson and his wife weren't ready for an extra person, not then. Lately they'd hoped to conceive another one, a keeper. But whatever chemistry had worked so well to spite them would not be charmed back. For months they tried to sidle up on luck, then gave themselves over to the humiliations of medical science. Neither the tiny incisions nor the Petri dish incubations did any good. Bad luck was all over them and stuck to them like a wad of gum, no matter how much they tried to scrape it off.

Nickerson saw the signs everywhere. Things disappeared around their house. Appliances broke. Moths ate holes in their clothing. They were dunned for back taxes owed on a queen-sized bed won in a drawing two years before. Nickerson considered giving the bed to Goodwill, but Francine wouldn't let him—it was a perfectly good bed. Now everything was compounded by the dog, as demonstrated by the hubcap.

Nickerson moved out of their nest of books and papers it had taken thirteen years to daub together. Something in there made him sneeze lately. He left behind everything, thinking that if he could start off fresh he could change his luck. His new apartment was white and bare with dark wooden floors and a fireplace with a fake log gas jet. Nickerson took to it like a cat, carefully walking around the perimeters of the rooms, peering out the edges of the windows. He furnished the place slowly, weighing everything in his soul to make sure it could do him no harm: two narrow chairs for his living room, a small white table for a desk.

Picking a bed was the hardest. For a time he slept in a sleeping bag on a foam pad. Nickerson considered their marriage bed the unluckiest thing he and Francine owned, the source of every unhappiness, as evidenced by the bill with interest due from the Internal Revenue Service. Finally he bought himself a futon and put it on the bedroom floor. After all, he was not a Boy Scout on an extended camp-out. He was an adult, and he bought the double size because he knew it was necessary to wish for love or else forever nullify the prospect. He made his night table from a sturdy wooden box. There were other additions, lamps and pots and pans, but mostly Nickerson looked on his apartment where the light slanting through the blinds shone on the sauce pan in the dish drain, and he saw it was good.

If you could peek through his window and see him sitting in one of his stiff straight chairs reading a library book with his cheap radio on the floor beside him, you might think him a lonely man. Surrounded by a fortress of superfluous things, we imagine ourselves made whole by sheer accumulation of records and books, utensils with matching handles, heirlooms and hand-me-downs, and the insurance policies and paper bags that come along with such stuff. But what if every little thing gathers loneliness to it?

Consider Francine, living back in their old place. All the pain and loneliness she felt smothered by, she signed over to Nickerson. She felt sure Nickerson suffered from walking bare floors without any slippers.

She got his number from Directory Assistance and called to invite herself over. When he told her no, she invited him back to their old house for dinner. He turned that down too. Francine couldn't understand any of this. No matter how well-meant their affection might be, they could only cause each other pain, Nickerson told her with regret. She could hear it in his voice, the regret, but mistook it for buried-away love that would grow back once Nickerson gave up this new craziness. She sent him a replacement hubcap through the mail, but he sent it back. He couldn't accept it.

Nickerson could have replaced it himself if that were all there was to it. Everybody knew the Hubcap House out on old Route 52, where every conceivable design hung on the fence or was nailed on the house like siding. He'd seen the owners loafing around their front porch, pleased with themselves and their creation. But he reflected that every one of those hubcaps had come free of somebody's car out on the highway, none of them rightly the property of the shifty denizens of Hubcap House.

Instead, he decided to take up walking. His wasn't a walker's town, though, but a town made by coal and steel. The rail yard stretched down by the river, and wind blew the gritty coal dirt up over the town. Nickerson walked through neighborhoods where the road had been widened by shearing away front yards, where cars went by too fast and too close. These houses were made of brick, made when people expected to live in a house forever. But some were derelict and all needed some repairs. When had everybody left this town? Somehow he'd missed it.

Nickerson mistrusted the sky and always walked with his wind-breaker and golf umbrella. He became a recognized figure to the car-loads of kids with nothing to do but prowl.

"Mr. Umbrella!" they screamed, and the words, always catching him by surprise, hit him with the force of a thrown object. "Umbrella Man!" He saw that this group's car was the same 1974 Chevrolet Chevelle as his own. But while his was a white four-door sedan, theirs was the coupe. It rumbled and rode lower to the ground, and its patchy finish of gray and brown turned it sinister as a warplane. The kids laughed and their car emitted a series of grunts and squeals as it went off down the street crabwise.

And so expecting rain, and knocked out of balance by taunting, he found himself one day seeking peace in Dwight's Eat-In-Your-Car Restaurant. In happier days, people pulled their cars under the long canopies to order from speakerphones. Now the lot was almost empty. No curb service now, no foot-long chili dogs and root beer floats.

Nickerson took a seat in a brown Naugahyde booth with a yellow Formica table. A small plastic case offered juke box tunes for selection from his booth, but Nickerson recognized few of the singers or songs. When his waitress came, he asked her, "How long have you lived here?"

"All my life," she told him, sounding the long flat vowels of the true mountain native.

"What happened to the people who used to live on Tenth Avenue?"

"Oh Lord. Way back." Her eyes darted around the room, looking for some clue to find her way through all the years that had gotten away. "They moved out way back when they widened the street, everybody who could. I was just a little girl."

Later Ruby Lail would be reminded of an old episode of *The Twilight Zone* where an android complete with a handsome plastic skin had been endowed with the twenty-year-old memories of his maker's hometown. The poor thing got loose in the world and found his way back to a place he thought was his own. But everything was all wrong. Still, because it was TV, the android fell in love with a human. But it could never work out, could it? Somehow he knew, somehow he had to get back to his maker and straighten this all out. Except he was hit by a car and found later on the road, a mess of wires and blinking lights where his muscles and veins should have been.

For his part, Nickerson was thinking about this place, Dwight's Eat-In-Your-Car, when its canopies may have covered turquoise and canary-yellow cars, when curb girls brought your barbecue on a tray that snapped right on the window, when the world was bright as chrome.

Neither Ruby Lail nor any of the women who worked at Dwight's was of an age to put on short pants and roller-skate to your car. And the beautiful cars of Nickerson's youth had all gone to rust. As much as he might like to go back, he could not. He knew that. But he accepted refill after free refill of his coffee, and when he finally reached his home that evening, sensed an emptiness in his apartment that had not been there before.

Nickerson didn't like to talk about his work; he was an accountant by trade. He kept the books of a half dozen businesses in town and did people's taxes in the spring. The episode of the bed was deeply embarrassing to him. It was free, but it was income. How had he neglected to report it? He simply forgot, and his absent-mindedness gnawed at him every time he looked at the long bank of file cabinets that were the all of his business. What else had he forgotten? What deadlines slipped by unnoticed, what new changes in laws and codes was he neglecting? The rotten luck of his married life could be contagious.

He took whatever steps he could. He never took work home; he never spoke of his personal life to Miss Edna, the elderly woman who answered his phone and made pleasant talk with his waiting clients. When the separation was imminent, he removed Francine's picture from his desk. Of course Miss Edna noticed, but said nothing.

Getting rid of the picture had been another matter. He carried it out under his jacket, frame and all, but when he looked at his wife's clear blue eyes of confident expectation, he knew he could not slide it down the side of the greasy dumpster in the alley. He carried it home and locked it in the trunk of his car. Maybe by keeping his rotten luck localized in this way, he would be able to contain it.

"Car in the shop?" Ruby Lail finally asked him one morning while taking down his order for breakfast. Nickerson's life had always run to habits; now he consciously cultivated them. Habits guaranteed a certain amount of order. His latest was breakfast at Dwight's, always arriving at 8:15 sharp, always selecting the same booth. Ruby got so she anticipated his turning the corner by the Handi-Mart and had his coffee and menu in place on the table.

Nickerson noticed Ruby Lail had brown eyes that sparkled and two front teeth with a funny overlap. He wondered if her eyes sparkled just for him. But after their initial conversation, he'd gone about establishing himself as one of those customers who grunts over his paper. Now he could find no course of action to slowly draw her out. He had to be careful, didn't want to play the fool.

Ruby Lail looked at Nickerson and saw a guy who was recently divorced. Soon he would say something that could be taken two ways and watch how she reacted. She hadn't been a waitress seven years and learned nothing. What other kind of man comes to breakfast day after day alone and looks at you when you take his order like he could put his head in your lap and cry?

Ruby Lail knew a few things about cars too, about how your transmission could lock up and your car could sit for months in your cousin's yard while he went through old pastures full of junk looking for a pretty good replacement. She knew about that and raising two kids in a mobile home on a waitress's pay. Whatever Nickerson took her to be when she made her dimpled smile, Ruby Lail was also a practical kind of woman.

She wasn't surprised to find Nickerson's business card on the table with her tip. *I can help you with your taxes*, he'd written on the back. It was getting to be that tax time of year. Fine, she thought, because she always took hers to H&R Block when they set up their booth in the mall, always left them, thinking they'd either messed up or crooked her.

On his way to his office Nickerson saw a hubcap, shiny side down, barely visible in the road next to the sidewalk. It was dark down there where the road passed under the railroad bridge, but he was able to see well enough to hook the tip of his umbrella into the hole cut into the hubcap to accommodate the valve stem. He took the hubcap up and propped it against the concrete stanchion next to the road. It was conical with a series of black rays leading out to its rim, vaguely suggesting a flying saucer. Nickerson angled it to catch the light from the street beyond and went on his way. He was pleased with himself, and was even more pleased a day later when it had disappeared. Somehow he was sure it found its way back to its rightful owner.

On her day off Ruby Lail took her collected papers down to Nickerson's office. She kept everything in a manila envelope, its back carefully lined to record fifty-two weeks of tips. The office was above a downtown Western Auto store. Nickerson had paneled the old plaster walls and furnished the place with bright plastic chairs and a coffee table full of magazines designed to radiate a dull honesty. He understood what people wanted in an accountant.

Despite the copies of *Field and Stream* and *Reader's Digest*, and even though Miss Edna kept some plants around to brighten the place up, Ruby Lail thought it as fearsome as a dentist's office. Maybe the source of Ruby's fear was Miss Edna, who, looking at Ruby in her thin nylon blouse and polyester skirt, judged her an adulteress, for the woman behind the unhappy ruin of Nickerson's gentle wife. Miss Edna had sent cuttings from her plants to Mrs. Nickerson on several occasions. Nickerson always assured her those shoots had grown into thriving healthy plants. She didn't know now whether she should believe him or not.

Ruby Lail tried to hold tight to her hope. She knew nothing about money, and thought Nickerson might brighten her financial outlook. Like most of us who've never quite had enough, she was mystified by wealth. It seemed like folks either had a lot and bought whatever they wanted, or bought Cost Cutters at the grocery and stayed alert for hidden charges. All the world's money had been divided up long ago. If you didn't have any now, your only chance was in lotteries and quiz shows. But she had read enough to know that unhappiness followed quickly on the heels of big winnings. Judging by such tales of waste and despair, Ruby wondered if it wasn't better to be poor. In this office, subjected to the stale air of thousands of calculations, she felt a little faint and asked Miss Edna if she couldn't open a window. By the time she sat down across from Nickerson, she simply asked, "How much is this going to cost me?"

"Nothing. This is strictly *pro bono*, free."

She smiled out of politeness and slid the envelope to him. And she answered his questions: name, address, Social Security number, and so on. As she did, she was thinking he was getting what he wanted, that here was another instance of hidden costs. "Why are you doing this?"

Nickerson thought about playing dumb. He could pretend she meant why some aspect of the procedure, not the larger question, *why?* He smiled, shrugged. He had no answer.

"Well, thanks. Only I wouldn't want you to think there was anything else . . . you know." She didn't look at him when she spoke, but ran her finger along the edge of his desk.

"Sure," he said. "No."

"I mean you don't know anything about me." Nickerson agreed. But didn't he know almost everything important there was to know about Ruby Lail?

After she left his office, though, Nickerson found himself growing angry. What did she think, they would do it on his desk or something like that? He paced and stewed. But he finally admitted he did have something sexual in mind, only his plan called for a longer and more tangled path along which Ruby might eventually forget where it was they started. How did he let this happen? God knows, Ruby Lail was still a pretty woman. But how had he allowed himself to wander from her friendly words, a little blessing given in return for payment of his tab, to high hopes for erotic possibilities? He had watched her slip with casual grace among the retired railroad men, filling and refilling their cups, stopping to listen to their clumsy jokes, teasing them back. She called them "sweetie" and "honey" and treated each one like he was her own silver-haired daddy. Nickerson realized they were just a bunch of lonely old men.

And Ruby was firm and strong looking. He understood. And he considered his own odd mixture of desire and a hollow emptiness that needed filling up. Like a junior high kid, he told himself. He took her envelope and looked over her weekly tallies on the back, dumped her check stubs, a W-2, a few receipts for prescriptions on his desk. This would be easy enough; he'd just do it so he could give her a completed return in the morning and that would be the end of it. It only took him a minute to enter her income for the year.

Like most accountants, Nickerson always voted Republican. But the figure he brought down to the gross adjusted income line shocked him. He considered his single income, or that from Francine's teaching, or even that of Miss Edna, which was next to nothing since Miss Edna already drew Social Security, and he measured them all against Ruby Lail and her two dependents. He could not imagine how she made it.

Nickerson took up his umbrella, locked the door, and started home. He had managed to work out a routine where he swung by a mom and pop grocery to pick up something for his dinner, by the library to get another book when he needed one. His car hadn't been driven in weeks. There it sat in the street, looking more and more like a hulk. Birds shat on it, rising sap dripped on it, a light film of coal dirt wrapped the whole thing. Seeing it droopy and dirty, he suddenly felt sorry for it, as if through his neglect the car had been insulted in a personal way. Hadn't he planned to let it sit there until it turned to rust?

He went in, cooked some hamburger meat, and mixed it up with macaroni and cheese. When he tried to get back into his book, an espionage thriller where the fate of the Free World dropped into the hands of one concerned citizen, he found it tedious. He stared at his phone and willed somebody to call him.

Nobody did, of course. He should have thought of a particular person, but who? He picked up the phone and dialed Francine. She was skittish and shy. "Are you alone?" he asked her.

"Me and Beanie"—their fat old cat—she told him, "and a stack of research papers." He should have known better.

"Those again," he said.

"Same old thing."

He could feel her waiting on the other end, doodling furiously with one of the colored pencils she used for her grading, making spiraling tornado funnels down the margin of some student's paper. "Hey, Francine, did you ever teach a Ruby Lail?"

"Is she the one?" she asked him. He had always sworn there was no-body. She knew she should believe him, it was just that nothing else he said made much sense. "Oh, this town is full of Lails. They say there are smart Lails and dumb Lails. I hope you at least picked a smart one."

"She's a client."

Francine hated herself when she started apologizing. She tried to stop and found herself getting even farther out of bounds. "Are you eating right? Are you still walking everywhere? Don't you want one of these TV sets?" All wrong, all wrong, she knew. Francine was a tall slim woman, a beautiful woman, but all the grace had been sprung out of her, and she hadn't been able to wish it back.

Nickerson hung up. He paced his apartment until he couldn't bear it anymore, then went outside and climbed in his car. He had to pump the accelerator, but it still started; it hadn't been sitting that long. And he drove. Maybe he imagined he drove aimlessly, but he managed to pass the Paint Lick Trailer Park, identified on Ruby Lail's 1040 only as Route 3, Box 161-A. The trailers climbed the hill on an old piece of pastureland like giant and impossibly steep stairs. Without being able to locate her name anywhere in the bank of mailboxes by the highway, Nickerson somehow sensed she lived in this place.

Inside her trailer with her kids asleep and the TV off, Ruby Lail felt a passing chill. She thought of Nickerson, a nice man really. She had no call to think terrible things about him; it was possible that somebody in this world would do something nice for you and expect nothing in re-turn. Possible. Then she thought of the android with the flawless plas-tic skin and of love and of its inevitably unhappy entanglements. "Lord, Lord," she said and resigned herself to her true feelings.

Handling somebody else's finances was usually an exhilarating feel-ing for Nickerson, like playing bridge for money or betting big on a bowl game. Now he simply felt stumped. The galling part about Ruby Lail's tax situation was that she would actually have to pay the IRS some money. Her pitiful pile of medical bills and household expenses didn't amount to a hill of beans, as Ruby herself might say. All Nickerson's tal-ent for pushing deductions to the limit without drawing an audit was pretty much useless here. He knew he wasn't being stupid and over-looking something. Ruby Lail's tax form was most likely the easiest one he'd fill out this year. The unfairness of it all was blunt as a hammer.

Nickerson had to do something with his guilt. He got up early and took his car around to the Robo wash and let the soapy water pour over it, watched the big woolly brushes cleanse the accumulated grime away. He spent seventy-five cents on the vacuum. The wash had been a good idea. For a short while he felt much better, until his mind got around to the presence of Francine's picture stashed in the trunk. He took the car back to his apartment, put it in the garage his rent was paying for, and walked to breakfast.

Along the way Nickerson found another hubcap spun all the way into one of the dusty yards on Tenth Street. It was smooth and spare with only a trademark etched in its middle. He turned its face toward the road and went on.

"Do you believe in luck?" he asked Ruby Lail. She was stiff and servile all through his breakfast, and it pained Nickerson to know it was all on his account, a favor gone wrong.

"I guess you make your own luck," she told him.

Of course! How obvious! Any sportscaster in America could have told him that. Except Nickerson had put so much time into his complex and secret theories of luck and lucklessness that a brief flash of enlightenment wasn't about to wreck months of his carefully circumscribed misery.

Maybe he wasn't so cockeyed. Contrary to what Ruby Lail believed, the world's money was in constant flux. Even in this town, where the big money had dried up and blown away, Nickerson could pick out the signs that identified the recently rich and the newly fallen. It was as simple as flashy new cars and worn-out shoes. Based on his observations, Nickerson concluded there was no logic, certainly no justice, so why not look at it as luck?

He fingered the envelope containing Ruby's completed 1040 form and thought about asking her if she made her own luck how she'd managed to manufacture something as rotten as this. But he didn't; he just said he was sorry he couldn't do anything for her.

Ruby Lail had expected as much, but turned white when she saw the hundred and thirty dollars she owed in taxes. How much was that in quarter tips from retired brakemen? Add in a few businessmen's dollars. She didn't have it.

There really is a Dwight, a man filled with the milk fat of a million double-thick shakes, oozing the grease of ten thousand cheeseburgers. He comes around at closing time, leaving his Coupe DeVille to idle as he picks up the receipts and checks the register. Otherwise, he leaves everything to his girls, those honest and responsible women who keep him going. He isn't ungrateful; he loves his girls and gives them huge boxes of candy and smoked hams for their Christmas bonuses, and pats their bottoms in a fatherly way whenever he gets a chance. He even advances their pay whenever it's necessary.

Ruby could get a couple of hundred from Dwight and have him draw it out of her check at the rate of eleven dollars a week for every ten he'd lent her. It wasn't that she felt Dwight unfair; interest had been a way of life in her family as long as she could remember, from the corner grocery store to all the department stores that would put your Christmas presents on layaway or sell you a couch or a TV or refrigerator on easy terms.

At Dwight's, hardly a week goes by without one of the girls slamming dishes around, looking for her coat and pocketbook, railing against Dwight and shitty tippers and that rough place on the edge of the counter that always picks your clothes. Ruby understood that what you lost when you owed your boss was the right to tell him to take his job and take a hike, the right to settle up at the end of any bad day and start over someplace else. She put off asking Dwight for a loan.

How, you might wonder, would a girl get herself stuck working at Dwight's-Eat-In-Your-Car Restaurant or at any of the other places just like it Ruby worked? Because, as it happens, Ruby Lail is one of the smart Lails, she and her sister Garnet, all those Lail girls working around town, all named after their birthstones. Love is stronger than good sense. Love will get you knocked up in high school and keep you too busy to earn a GED.

Up to now, Nickerson had been careful. He'd kept his apartment as antiseptic as the day he moved in. The walls were still bare, for example, since it was hard to guess what sort of effect a picture might have. He practiced kindness to all people and animals to ease the suffering of his wife and to mollify the rotting carcass of the dog. He had found five hubcaps and left them for their owners to reclaim. Whatever he decided to do about Ruby Lail most likely would change all that. Nickerson considered that sitting around thinking about her was liable to have the same effect on his luck as actually acting out his desires. He called her up at Dwight's.

Who knows all the ways love can go wrong? Ruby was taking her break, smoking a Salem out back behind the Dumpster, thinking about the ones she'd already found out—pretty men, dangerous men, men with money. Nickerson was none of those. He needed her; she could feel his need coming off him like the heat off the fry cook's grill. She thought he could be a dangerous man too, not like the more familiar kind, into drinking and driving and rough sex and finally hitting. Inside, somebody was hollering that the phone was for Ruby Lail.

At least she would get a good dinner for a change, Ruby Lail thought. Then she put Nickerson off for a couple of days; she told him she had to make sure her sister could take care of her kids. She might as well find out whether he was going to be more than another divorced and horny guy. He could pick her up outside Dwight's on Friday.

"*Pro bono* doesn't mean for free, it means for the public good, *pro bono publico*," Ruby Lail told Nickerson when she climbed in his car. She'd gone home and looked it up.

"Oh," Nickerson said. He didn't know; it was something he'd heard lawyers say on their lunch breaks. He tried to think of something else to say, but Ruby Lail tongue-tied him. She wore a red dress made out of some sort of acetate material—Nickerson thought it must be inflammable—black stockings with a rhinestone flower set around her ankle bone, and black, impossibly high heels. Her cheeks were rouged and angry, her eyelids painted an iridescent green.

They drove in silence toward their destination, a steak place in an old water-powered mill. Nickerson chose it for its discreet distance from town and because he kept the books for its owner. Ordinarily he got his meal at a discount. He felt the sensation that the car was slipping out of his control. The streets were full of broken glass and potholes. Other drivers routinely ran through yellow and red lights. The simple decorum of stop and yield had been abandoned for a more savage system of daring and will.

As they were coming to the spot where he struck the dog, Nickerson was moved to speak. "I guess I often think about the difficulty of love. I mean long-term love. Maybe everybody does when they get older. You know?" He glanced in Ruby's direction, but she was looking fiercely down the highway. "Hormones don't make you do as many stupid things as they used to." He stopped again. "Or maybe they still do. . . ."

Ruby Lail waited to sneak a glance until he was taking a curve and couldn't meet her eyes. He looked as fatherly as Fred McMurray in his navy blue cardigan and button-down shirt. "Are you talking about your divorce?" she asked him. "Or something else?"

Nickerson told her about his wife's abortion, how he considered it the event that signaled the end of his marriage even though it happened eleven years ago.

"My momma says a baby is a gift from God," Ruby Lail told him.

"Is it?"

"Well, yeah." Except, she was thinking, it's a funny kind of gift to give a kid. She was thinking how Nickerson, despite the wardrobe of a television father, was innocent of how the world really worked. "It must be nice," she told him, "to be able to put your finger on a reason like that."

"What about you?" he asked her.

For her it was a long ugly job, like mopping up a dirty nasty floor, like cleaning up after a stinky senile old man. There was no end to the fights and no money and sick babies and nowhere to go. As he listened, Nickerson felt like he was being pushed against the driver's side door. "Mister, you don't know what bad luck is," Ruby Lail told him.

In the gathering dark Nickerson saw only two reflected yellow disks as the possum stepped over the white line on the edge of the highway. He mashed on the brake and pulled the wheel hard to the right.

The woody West Virginia hills are full of thick juicy roots, nuts, and tender berries, so why would any animal take a notion to cross a major U.S. highway? Love. Possums, skunks, coons, they can't leave it alone. Finally, they all have to cross the road in search of another of their own kind to love.

Nickerson thought the car spun around three or four times. Ruby Lail, who had more experience at this sort of thing, knew it was only once. She didn't try to correct his misapprehension. They'd come to rest in a field where soft mud pushed up to the rocker panels. The main question was how to get out.

When he put his foot into the goo, Nickerson was wondering if he would ever reach some solid ground. The mud tried to suck his shoes off at every step. Finally, he came up on the shoulder of the road, went immediately back to the skid marks. Tears of relief came to his eyes as he looked on this miracle of empty highway. There was no dead animal; he'd missed it.

"Well?" Ruby Lail surprised him. She'd kicked off her shoes and shucked off her pantyhose and left them in the car. Nickerson looked at her bare muddy legs and felt his world shifting unexpectedly. And maybe for the better.

He was right. A bank of fog lights hit them as a snorting black pickup truck equipped with oversized wheels and a winch rolled up out of the night. Out hopped a short-legged boy in a ball cap who'd been waiting all these months since he bought that winch for some honest reason to use it. With no concern for his fancy cowboy boots, the kid waded into the field and groped in the mud to fix his hook around the frame of Nickerson's car. It came out of the field reluctantly, like a fish tired of fighting.

When his car was back on the roadside and running, Nickerson was moved to open his wallet, but the boy waved his hand and said he would take nothing for his work. In an instant he was only a diminishing roar down the highway.

What's the advantage in being the Lone Ranger, in tipping your hat and riding off alone with only your self-satisfied humility to keep you company? Meanwhile, the grateful sodbuster embraces his wife, and an odd transference takes place. All that gratitude and goodwill and love of all humankind must be shared just between the two of them. There's nobody else around.

It's just as well that Nickerson and Ruby Lail never made it to the expensive steak place. She would have ordered hers well-done and picked fries instead of the baked potato. She wouldn't have liked Nickerson's expensive wine; he would have ended up ordering her a Coke.

Instead, Ruby Lail thought she should take off her makeup along with her stockings and shoes, and later she would rinse the sticky clay off her legs while sitting on the edge of Nickerson's tub. It had been hours since Nickerson considered the state of his luck at all.

Francine was home that night, sitting in a La-Z-Boy recliner with a TV tray on her lap, grading a set of themes on an open topic. She read, *Your standards may be too high. There are many clean and friendly people out there looking for love. Give them a chance.* She started laughing, thought this was a line she'd have to share with Nickerson, laughing so hard she cried, and then she wasn't laughing at all.

She had fallen in love with Nickerson for his gentleness and humility. He made a practice of feeding the birds in their backyard. But when she recalled the accident involving the dog, she saw her husband walking along the highway with the black tool hanging from his hand. Stooped a little, he had the aspect of a lower-order primate. He could strike the dog on the base of the skull if it were necessary. Long ago he had driven her two hundred miles across the state line and deep into Ohio for her abortion. Francine realized it was unfair to put all the blame on him; she had wanted it too. It hadn't been hard to dispose of that little lump of flesh; they both believed they could always get another. She thought of the would-have-been child with regret, but only because they failed so many times to get another had she turned to anger and remorse.

In the end she'd thrown things: a spatula, a turkey sandwich that flew to pieces as it crossed the kitchen, a can of tomato juice. Only the last could possibly have hurt him, but to strike out at Nickerson was like beating the air. He hadn't been present long before he got around to leaving the house.

She called his office where he kept an answering machine. Miss Edna's voice greeted her on behalf of Nickerson, offered his prompt service, honesty, and integrity.

"Nickerson, you bird feeder, dog killer. You humane bastard. You treat me like a fish flopping around in the bottom of a boat. Why don't you put me out of my misery?" Francine pushed the button to break the connection. Ugh, how humiliating, but she couldn't erase it. She called back. "I'm sorry. I still love you. I'm sorry, Miss Edna, too, you had to hear my cursing."

Propped up in his futon, his room illuminated by the mercury vapor light on the corner, Nickerson contemplated his simple furnishings. Up till now, they had done the trick. But he considered Ruby Lail, who kissed recklessly, who purred like a sleek comfortable cat, who made such pleasurable love. He considered the long drive out to her place, the moon face of a child he was sure he'd seen at the window as he pulled away, the chilly ride home. And he remembered his ex-wife-in-the-making, Francine, her sheet and flannel gown twisted around her. He felt joy and pain commingled, and embraced them both. His life had reached a new level of complexity. From his bed at this moment, he felt like he was capable of understanding all of it.

If Ruby Lail could afford it, she'd have called in sick. Not because she really was sick—she had a hell of a headache was all—but because she knew she couldn't face Nickerson so soon for breakfast. Ruby Lail could tell you it's easy to hire a waitress in a town full of out-of-work men. That thought was enough to get her out of bed in the morning. Besides, she had to pee and could feel the diaphragm pushing inside her belly. Last night, as he'd driven off, she stood just inside the door listening for her kids, hearing instead the loose gravel popping under his tires. She felt a draft blowing up her bare legs, and it all seemed strangely familiar. Nickerson was just like that android, just as lost, just as confused. No, it wasn't seeing him at breakfast, but the chance of not seeing him that scared her.

As long as Nickerson had been there, Francine managed schoolteaching just fine. She wore her hair short so the gray hardly showed, concentrated on looking radiant and unflappable in the face of her students' teenaged angst, her colleagues' middle-aged bitterness. Now she got runs in her stockings; her hair, grown longer, worked loose from its clasp. She stood in the hallway and peered in on the biology teacher's movie on predation. As the wolves tore into the moose flesh, she felt what it would be like if her students sensed her weakness. Francine tried to hang on to her love for Nickerson.

But Francine couldn't guess how he'd betrayed her. In addition to her abortion, Nickerson told Ruby Lail about the dog and the hubcap, and the other hubcaps he'd found in the street, and about his belief that through such rituals of contrition he would find absolution. Ruby took it all in, but he couldn't guess what effect it had on her. She just kissed him.

It was Nickerson who'd suggested pouring a little bourbon into the Diet Cokes. Now in the dull daylight he found his moment of enlightenment had slipped away. Maybe it's just that a long night is the best time for such an illusion, when the only sound is the noise of tires sucking against the dewy pavement, when the streetlight makes all shadows long and romantic.

He decided Ruby Lail thought he was a fool. And looking at his apartment, he saw for himself—the bed on the floor, the bare cupboards and closets, the small desert scene he'd ripped from a magazine in his office and taped to the wall above his white table. "What are you, a monk or something?" Ruby asked him.

What made her marvel was that a man who could have everything— nice clothes, a good car—would empty his life out so. Not having enough unhappiness, he'd gone looking for more.

Maybe he'd found it. He overslept and found himself facing the options of skipping breakfast and remaining true to his regime of walking to work, or taking his car and stopping in Dwight's as usual. Sure, the whole notion of luck and contrition was silly. Whose system is not when its foundation of unsubstantiated miracles, unconfirmed sightings, and private revelations is finally exposed? Nickerson's overhauled luck had proved itself reliable to him so far, but now, to be true to his vague beliefs, he needed to act, and there was no right action.

Miss Edna called from the office and told him in a choking voice that she was quitting. Nickerson drove straight there without stopping at Dwight's. There he found Miss Edna banging around the waiting room like a panicked bird that'd flown in the window by mistake. She had already placed what plants would fit into boxes from the Western Auto downstairs. Nickerson offered to drive her home if she'd only tell him what was wrong. She pushed the button on the answering machine and held her ears.

Nickerson shut it off as quickly as possible. It may have been the swearing that upset Miss Edna so, but Nickerson heard the pitch of Francine's voice. It sounded like a woman who would stuff her pockets full of river rocks, wade into the dirty Ohio, and let the water do its work.

Ruby Lail's cousins, the Dumb Lails, live in Hubcap House. They'll sell you one, though they always seem reluctant. While it's possible to comb their collection, including the bushel baskets full of hubcaps sitting around the place that they haven't yet bothered to hang up on the house, and come up with a full set, most people go there looking for a single replacement. They are surprised that the Lails want so much, but since they've already made the drive out there they always pay. Thanks to us, thanks to our craving for the trappings of order, the Dumb Lails don't even keep steady jobs.

Now, while Miss Edna was quitting Nickerson and Ruby was trying not to look frantic serving breakfast down at Dwight's, Francine turned from the chalkboard to find a boy in her first period class setting the sole of his sneaker on fire with a disposable lighter.

Nickerson's head was filled with the sounds of cars squealing away from traffic lights, of distant sirens, of the nearby sound of his own telephone which rang and rang, but which neither he nor Miss Edna could summon the will to answer. Nickerson felt that a stronger man, and wiser, would somehow take hold of the situation and act. Such men, though, stood in the open turrets of tanks or sat astride skittish horses that nonetheless obeyed them. Did they ever find themselves stuck in the middle of a nearly empty office cradling pots of African violets?

Nickerson carried Miss Edna's boxes of plants down the stairs to put them in his car. No matter what he said to Miss Edna, his words could not move her. "So bad, so bad" was all she could tell him. Nickerson took her babble to be a judgment on his recent behavior distilled into Francine's message. When he shifted the last box to his hip and unlocked the trunk, there she was, Francine, staring at him through the busted glass in the picture frame. He closed the lid and put the plants in the back seat.

When Francine tried to reprimand the boy with the burning shoe, she slapped her. Maybe he was trying some new kind of drug, who knows? But as she sat in the principal's office crying, the man could think of nothing to do but call Nickerson at work. How could he guess they were separated?

By now it couldn't matter. Nickerson knew he moved at the goad of his deserved retribution. Back from Miss Edna's daughter's place where he stayed to see her put to bed with milk and a Valium, where he forced himself to stand in the woman's accusatory glare, Nickerson took the principal's call.

He drove Francine home, to what used to be their home. He brewed her tea, finding the tea things—the pot with the broken and glued-back handle, the perforated ball—where they had always been. Going to the upstairs closet, he found her a quilted comforter. But the sight of these familiar objects, the comfortable closeness of the narrow halls with their worn wood floors, did not move him. As soon as Nickerson could convince himself Francine was calmed and resting, he left. He was sure she would be all right.

Only then did he think maybe he should stop back by Dwight's and tell Ruby Lail about his day. On the way, right around the Handi-Mart on the corner of Eighth Street and Tenth Avenue, Nickerson saw a hubcap. Its outside ring was smooth and shiny bright, the next section stamped out to give the appearance of stiff wire spokes; nearer the middle was another ring of spun aluminum and inside that a hexagon of bright red reflective plastic which contained, molded right into the disk, a golden Chevrolet emblem. Nickerson recognized the hubcap as his own.

At that moment he felt affirmed. In his heart, he always knew he would find it. Forever afterwards, he would recall the guy pumping his own gas at the self-serve island, the aimless kid loitering along the sidewalk, drivers passing in their cars, all turning toward his special moment. The sky would always be high and clear, the air sharp with spring.

Across the way, Ruby held her coffee pot suspended above a customer's empty cup and watched as Nickerson pounded the hubcap into place with his bare hand. The wind kicked up the dust in the street; low clouds scudded across the tops of buildings. It would rain soon, rain hard.

––––––––––––

Nickerson would take Ruby Lail to concerts and plays. He would buy her clothes made of 100 percent cotton and virgin wool. He would buy her children educational toys. Somehow, he would never feel she loved him. He had glimpsed a moment; where had it slipped away?

It would never occur to him that Ruby had made a call to her cousins, the Dumb Lails, and had that hubcap left in the street for him to find. That she went around work all morning watching out for it, making sure the wrong person didn't stop and pick it up. If Dwight had been around, she might have lost her job. Finally she had gone over and given one of the stoned kids who hung around the Handi-Mart three dollars to watch it.

Maybe if he had found in his heart a way to see these things, his luck might have turned out differently. Ruby Lail's kids would have run to him and hugged onto his legs when he came through the door to fetch her. Francine would no longer have needed to visit the psychologist twice a week. His life would have tumbled to the unadulterated *yes* on some big cosmic slot machine. But Nickerson couldn't figure any of this.

It seemed like his luck flowed, for good or ill, like water from a rock, and one day it just stopped.

It was like getting over a cold. He bought a television and VCR, a comfortable chair to read in, and a matching couch. Matching dishes with a little blue border and copper-bottomed pots. Nothing startling happened in his life. His symptoms had quietly left him; it took him a while to notice. But when he did, he hired a group of Boy Scouts willing to wash and wax his car.

Whether hubcaps might still be found in the gutters and tall weeds didn't matter; he stopped looking for them. If there were signs to be read in the dead dogs along the highway, Nickerson could no longer find them. All around him, people who loved him were in pain. He saw it now.

When the Hoot Owl Moves Its Nest

There are spirits living in this world. There are people in this town who can contact them, who read the signs and know what will happen on down the road. Hunkies from the Old Country and black folks and old hillbillies who haven't been taken in by city ways. I study those people and listen.

The old fart who lives across the way is one of them. He comes over when he sees me sitting out by the kitchen door, always carrying his coffee cup. "Here," I tell him, "let me get you something to liven that up." That's what he wants.

I go in the house, being careful to let the screen door bang shut behind me and squeak all the floor boards on my way to the living room. Stopping in the doorway, I snort like a pig to let my daughter and that boy all piled up in the corner of the couch know what I think of their doings. I see their shirttails bagging, that pink skin around their collars. "It's a pretty night out," I tell them, "You all look like you could use a little air." The gal looks at me through slitty eyes. That's all right, they think they know what passes for happiness nowadays.

In other days, was it anything different? When I was their age I don't remember giving it much thought one way or the other. Once I was on the high school football team and broke my ankle, and it made me happy as hell to be done with practice on that muddy field.

I go on off to the basement and get the whiskey I keep slid down beside the coal furnace in the summertime and pour a good slug for the old fart and one for myself into my tea glass, then take a pull off the bottle before I go back outside. "You can keep a secret, can't you?" I ask him before I hand his coffee back. He's been drinking my whiskey for fifteen years.

He grins. "When's a secret not a secret anymore?" Hell, I don't know.

I have seen signs myself, but I couldn't figure them. There was this time once when a bunch of us went fishing down on Claytor Lake. This was before it was so built-up, before so many people owned houses along the lakeshore so you feel now like you're fishing on somebody's front yard. We had an old trailer house pulled up down there that we used to stay in, usually a bunch of us engineers and surveyors from work. But this time I took the old lady and the boy, our first kid who was still in diapers, and an old boy I worked with, Skeeter, and his wife.

Skeeter was a big talker, and I kind of liked working with him. We were surveying for Powell Coal then. They gave us a car and gas and what all, and we just lit out for the woods every day. I kept a shotgun in the car and would get a pheasant or quail every now and then. The company didn't care as long as we showed we'd done some real work by the end of the week. Half the time they didn't even know what county we were in.

While we drove along Skeeter would tell me all these stories about fish he'd caught. I knew they were lies, but hell, he told them so good I had to listen. Finally I said, "Let's go fishing, me and you." He didn't much want to. He hadn't been married long. Shirley and me, we'd gotten married right after I came back from Korea. Everybody was doing it, and we did too—though that's a mistake I'll tell you about in a minute. But he had just got married to this little gal who worked downstairs in the big company office—in the stores division, just another secretary, but real pretty. I could see how come he might not want to miss a night with her.

So I said, "Me and the old lady might look all broke down, but we still know how to have a good time. We'll all go." I'm not sure he thought much of this idea either, but he was kind of stuck since that had been the thing that was holding him back, what to do about his wife and all.

We got over there just before dark on Friday and the trailer was a wreck. I guess it was always a wreck, it was just with two women along all the trash on the floor and the dirt sort of jumped out at me. The old lady had seen worse, I knew, but Skeeter's little gal, Joann, thought it was damned awful. So Shirley and me threw open the windows to let some air in and started piling up the dead soldiers and sweeping the place out. After about an hour it got to looking about as good as a place like that can look.

So I said, "What should we do?" And nobody said a thing. Finally Joann admitted she liked to play Rook. They had brought along a Rook deck. "My God," said the old lady, looking through the cards, "I bet I haven't played Rook since I was in the seventh grade." Joann got all red in the face, but we played anyhow. It's a simple kind of game. While I was dealing, the old lady jumped up and said, "How 'bout some beers?" And when nobody said a thing, she said, "Beers all around then." She always liked to take charge, the old lady.

We played probably forty hands of Rook, a big long tally sheet on the back of an old calendar stretching clean across the table. Shirley had been drinking some beer (I tell you this because of the way she treats me now, forgetting she used to get pretty thirsty herself once), and I had been having my share. Skeeter was coming along—being a good sport, the old lady called it, since he was losing at Rook too. But there was Joann. Hers was in a jelly glass with a picture of Abe Lincoln on one side and his log cabin home on the other, and she had not drunk a drop. It had sweated itself warm until the glass was sitting in a puddle, and Joann wouldn't even touch it to move it away from her.

The three of us were up and down all night long pissing. Then me and Skeeter went off in the boat around daybreak to see if we could get some fish. We were both using night crawlers and casting up toward the banks, but we didn't get a damned thing except some bream. There were some big ones, and they made a nice breakfast. The old lady came down to the lake and helped clean them while Joann stayed back at the place and watched our kid.

When we were running back in, though, we saw some splashing back up in a little cove. Skeeter wanted to take a look, but I'd fished enough for one day and I knew I would catch hell for being out so long as it was. "It's an old bullfrog or something," I told him. But I marked that place.

Already the shit was getting pretty deep in the trailer. Joann wasn't talking to any of us including Skeeter. I guess until last night she'd never seen him touch a drop. She messed her eggs around the plate and wouldn't have any of the fish. Starve then, damn you, I was thinking. But the old lady said since it was getting toward the middle of the day why didn't we go on over to the State Park and swim a little.

So we did and things were a little better with other people around and all. Shirley and Skeeter got in the water and swam out past the diving platform. The old lady loves to swim, or used to, I doubt if she could find a suit she could get into these days. And I guess I was glad to see her out there having a little fun. I had to stay back on the beach with the baby and Joann but, hell, somebody had to be with her, and I guess the old lady had done her share that morning. It felt like wintertime in Korea in that trailer when we walked in from cleaning those fish.

I said to Joann, "So you work down in the stores division?" and it was like I'd pushed a button. She turned her head in my direction and gave me this Miss America smile and started to blab about what it was like down there and Mr. Marsh and Mr. Burke and Miss Ellis. It wasn't like I didn't know any of them. Ray Marsh was the biggest bullshitter in Powell's Bottom and here this gal was talking about him like he was first cousin to Jesus H. Christ. I thought about Skeeter and the kind of lying he could do, just for fun or whatever, and I began to think I understood Joann.

The old lady and Skeeter got out of that lake where they had been for about an hour paddling around and something had changed. There she was being frisky with him, touching him on the arm and smiling.

You might see what I mean about signs. But seeing them can't tell you what to do. It's something I can't let go the older I get. They say you're put in this world supposed to do right, and then things happen. Maybe they're outside your control. Or maybe you can't help yourself. A sign ought to be put out there to help you.

That night when we played Rook all over again, Shirley was frisking again with the occasional rub up the forearm, a little footsie under the table. I was watching that shit. But we all (the three of us) drank a lot of beer again. And Joann was winning at Rook and telling us all about the poor old bastards she worked with in the stores division and so she was happy too.

The next morning Skeet didn't even roll over when I tried to get him out for fishing so I went on out by myself. We kept this little 12-foot johnboat over at the trailer with a five-horse fishing motor, and I was putting around the shoreline just looking at the lake and enjoying myself, feeling good to be out of that trailer, and not even considering right then my prospects for getting any fish, when I thought about that cove we'd gone by the day before. I opened out the throttle and headed over there.

Laid back in that shady shallow place were the two biggest bass I think I've ever seen. There they were just circling one another, swimming and swimming, and no more giving a damn if I was there than if I'd been a rock or tree. I thought I could catch both of these bastards if I just used the right thing. I had my night crawlers, but they hadn't done a thing for me yesterday. So I looked in my tackle—I had some plugs, some Jitterbugs and such, but I'd never had much luck on them. And I had some plastic worms. Plastic worms were the coming thing. Why I don't know. A fish is dumb, and I guess it's easy to get him to think he wants something kind of flashy. In that way he's no different from us. So I tied on a purple plastic worm with a propeller and a couple of orange beads in front of it and cast it just beyond where those fish were swirling around and reeled it back through them.

One fish turned on that worm as it went past him and chomped down on it like he could have bit it in two—since then I have heard tell of a feller catching a fish with half a plastic worm in its craw—but he didn't break it. I jerked like hell and set my hook, and that bastard took off. He tried to run for the bank and snag me up; he tried to run at me and get under the boat. He took off down the lake and tried to run me out of line. But I got him.

The other was still there swimming, so I went after him and he took that purple worm too. And he fought like hell, too. But finally I sat there with two 28-inch bass in my boat. When you catch a damned big fish, your first thought is to put him back. I can't say why. Any man who doesn't feel that way ought not be fishing. But I didn't put either one of them back. I wanted Skeeter to see these. I wanted him to see the difference between bullshit and honest to Christ fishing.

So I pulled the johnboat up on the bank right there and cleaned them, and that's when I realized they were a him and a her. And when all those eggs fell out, I knew they had been spawning.

Well, shit. There was no law against it, but I knew I'd done wrong. I looked up in the sky, expecting a big black cloud to come rolling up on me, but nothing happened. The sun was full up, and the lake was like a window glass.

Bonnie Maye—she's secretary to the chief engineer and a gal I like to have a cup of coffee with when I'm through the office—says everybody has to pay his bills sometime. Whenever you see somebody pulling some shit and looking like he's getting away with it, he's going to pay. It might be years from now, and he might never connect back to whatever it was that made him deserve it.

That's how she explains Ronnie Willoughby, who swapped out the snow tires on his company car for some old bald things he had around his place. A couple of years later he went off the road on Anawalt Mountain and broke both legs. It happened late in the summer, and it wasn't even raining. He never knew what hit him. Bonnie Maye did. She has a way of calling your attention to those things.

I started the motor and headed on back to the trailer house, and as I brought the boat into view, I felt less bad and more good, looking at those two fish laying at my feet. Old Joann was sitting down by the piece of dock we'd thrown up, looking kind of mournful, and I told myself I wasn't going to let her make me low, too, that this ought to be one of those mornings you remember the rest of your life.

"Lookie here," I said to her, "look at these damned fish. You'll never see any pair like that again." And she got up and came over. I could see her eyes were all smeary with tears now. "Oh hell," I said. "Where's Skeet? Where's Shirley?" She just shrugged, and I picked up the fish through their gills and took up my pole and started for the trailer, thinking I was the very picture of a first-class bass fisherman.

It was the way they were laughing that gave them away. Hell, they were dressed and all and having some coffee. But there's few times when the old lady's eyes will get the light in them like that. I knew what Joann was bawling about then.

There was a minute when I could have done something about it. I could have knocked the shit out of Skeeter or gone out of the cabin, got in the car, and drove off and left them. But that minute got away from me. I never knew exactly what they did; I never asked them. I had a notion, and as time went by I brooded on it until that notion got hardened into a real thing, something I could see plain as day when I closed my eyes and pictured it. Maybe I still do.

Finally the old lady said, "My God, Skeet, look at those fish." And they both started admiring the hell out of my fish like they really meant it. "We could cook one up and eat it right now," she said.

"It looks like you all done ate," I said. That was the first thing out of my mouth since I went in there so the words came out like I was a kid who got no Christmas.

"Well, boo hoo hoo," Shirley told me, but her face got red. Skeet laughed. He didn't catch on to it.

We might have been stuck there all day trying to act like nothing ever happened except poor old Joann came in and said she didn't feel so good and couldn't we go on home. It was the only thing she said all weekend that made sense.

When is a secret not a secret anymore? When everybody is in on it, I guess.

The old fart coughs a little and dangles his cup off the end of his finger. It's his little sign. I give him a wink and slide back into the house for some more whiskey, thinking I better be dropping back in on those lovebirds too.

The idea is for nobody to say anything. The idea is to see how many times I can slip down to the basement and climb back up those off-kilter stairs with no banister and go sit in front of the TV set with my daughter and that boy she's stuck on and make it seem like we're all acting natural.

Except every time I go in the front room I can feel how the air has heated up a couple of degrees, their faces all red and puffy lips, clothes getting all twisty around. I make a groan and drop down in my recliner. "Who done it?" I say, pointing the muzzle of my tea glass at the screen.

"Uh," the old boy is trying to answer until my daughter gives him a push. "Daddy!" the gal says, but her voice is slow and thick. A bunch of fat boys dressed up in bib overalls and checkered shirts are dancing with pitchforks.

"You all don't know the half of it," I tell them.

When I came back from the service I was broke; went in broke, came out broke. Went in to keep from having to go to work in the mines and came out and the mines was the only work I could get for a while. I was too broke to have a care; I was walking around in my service shoes and working in my combat boots. Here came Shirley driving her '46 Ford down the valley from over in McDowell County, making good money working as a nurse for the company doctor in Bishop. She had been a year ahead of me in school, and I wouldn't have a thing to do with her back before I left for the service. The only reason I started going with her this time was so I wouldn't have to thumb a ride to the movies. Only after the first date, when I tried to crawl all over her, she wouldn't see me except at her house.

I'm trying to think how I got to love her. I thought she had something all right. Not because she was from a better class of people. She was. Her momma had taught school, and her daddy was head engineer with the company when head engineer was something to be. But she just did whatever she wanted, it seemed like—smoked cigarettes, drank liquor straight out of the bottle, and drove that car all over creation. When it snowed, she'd put the chains on and go some more.

I'd go over to her daddy's house and sit with her on the couch, just like these two, with her old man sitting across from us acting like he was reading the paper. Every now and then he'd read out loud from the editorials against higher wages and say it was a damned shame we ever let the unions in the coal fields. I'd agree—hell, I didn't care. And so he decided I was all right and got me on with the surveyors.

Shirley came around, too, and decided I had suffered enough, that maybe we could try another movie. Afterwards, she drove us up the Falls Mills road and we parked in the pull-out beyond the second bridge. We did it, Shirley with her feet braced against the dashboard and me on my knees in the floorboards. Then while we were pulling our clothes back on and she was checking with a flashlight to make sure we hadn't left a stain on the seat, she told me, "I want you to marry me. I'm too old for screwing in cars."

I had been laid in a whorehouse when I was in the service once and that was all. But that's not my excuse. I wanted a cream and yellow two-door Chevrolet Deluxe and one of those TV sets. All around us people seemed to be wanting the same things, but it looked to me maybe only when you were married was it natural to actually get around to having them.

I won't lie. Those were good times. Once the old lady had what she wanted she let the string out a little. You've heard what they say about nurses. We swam naked out in Falls Mills Dam, diving under the water to hide from the lights whenever a car went by. She'd come out on dates with no underpants on, laughing when I found it out. I was a regular fool for her, and sometimes I think after it all went to hell I deserved what I got coming at me.

Now here's this old boy and gal, and I could sit around and devil them like Shirley's old man did me. Or I could let them alone. Let them get naked and see how it feels, do it until they're sweated up and satisfied. I could tell them there's no big mystery to it. I won't; I'll have another sip of whiskey instead.

The old fart is still here, squatting with his butt rested against the house waiting. He's just like me, what else does he have to do? Now he takes the whiskey straight, swishes it around his mouth a while and lets it go down slow. "Listen at your hoot owl," he says. And I do, hearing it call down toward the open end of the hollow. It used to stay back up behind the house where the bottomland runs up into the cleft of a couple of round hills. It's shifted its nest. "It's one of the old signs," the old man tells me.

"How do you account for what's happened to me?" I asked Bonnie Maye one time because about nine months after my and Skeeter's fishing trip to Claytor Lake that gal of mine was born.

"You know," she said, looking over her coffee cup with those big brown eyes. I did too, then. Bonnie Maye and me had some fun a time or two ourselves. We used to sneak into my sister's house for lunch hour — she lived just down the alley if you went out the office building the back way. Then I got caught by Mr. Chief Engineer himself feeling Bonnie up back in that storeroom where they keep the blueprints.

He had me into his office and raised hell with me in his college-man language, told me he'd fire me if he ever caught me at it again. "I been surveying for this company for five years," I told him, probably the stupidest thing I ever said in my life. "Stick to surveying, then," he told me.

That about tore it with Bonnie Maye and me. I slipped back around and tried to get her to see me again, but Mr. Engineer had talked to her some too. He was a Sunday school teacher, on top of everything else, and he fed Bonnie all this crap about did she want to be a woman taken in adultery and how Jesus didn't think much of that. That's all right, I thought, and spread it all over town that he was the one fucking Bonnie Maye.

It looked like I was getting the shitty end of the stick all the way around, and I didn't see how come it should have to be. What I thought was somebody had to pay, didn't they? When Bonnie finally did get married, she couldn't have any kids like she wanted and then she turned into a diabetic. Bonnie might say she paid too.

I consider it lucky, I guess, that tale I told never got back to her because we're still friends in a complicated way. Sometimes I look in her eyes and know she still thinks about those times up in Sis's bedroom, the sun coming through the curtains making the whole room pink. Bonnie Maye was sweet to me. I tell her I still love her, and she says that wasn't ever it. But it was. She says the best you can do is learn to accept how things are.

I want to think otherwise. The signs were always there for me to see and understand, and I flat missed them. Back on the lake, those two bass did everything they could but get up out of the water and talk. Maybe if they could, it all would be different.

After that weekend, what was there for me to do? I went to work on Monday, drove through town and there sat Skeeter on the bridge with his dinner bucket, waiting. We walked around in the woods all week over in McDowell County, me not saying a thing to Skeet except "Shut up," and "Pull the slack out of the chain," and "Hold that damned rod straight."

I thought a thing or two, though. One thing was, come fall I could carry my old shotgun into the woods like we always did and blow that boy's head off. It would be an accident, but you could say I'd been having accidents my whole life now, and everybody knew me for it. Make like we'd jumped a bird and I aimed a little low. Worst that could come of it would be I'd lose my job, but I wound up losing it anyway, and it wasn't much to lose. I could even see Skeeter laying stretched out in the woods, one arm thrown out in front of him, the other down by his side like he was trying to learn how to swim on dry land. Face down because I couldn't picture a man with no face on him or with blood all over the place instead of a face.

Then for a while, getting drunk seemed like the best idea to me. Things had gone about as far to shit as they could around the house. I could see the old lady's belly coming up bigger every damned day. But hadn't we done it ourselves a night or two before we drove over there and who's to say they got as far as fucking anyway? That baby gal got born regardless. A couple of years came and went, and I got so sick of looking at Skeeter I got him off my crew. The company paid to send Joann to school to learn computers, thinking computers were the coming thing and Joann would never leave Powell's Bottom ever. They were halfway right. Damned if Joann didn't read those want-ads and go off to Washington, D.C., where she could make four times the money, and take Skeeter with her.

Even with him not around to look at every day, I could see Skeet in that baby, in the hair that was not blond or brown but almost a dirty shade of green and those freckles on pasty white skin. I tried to take that baby in my arms and hold her close to me, but I never could do it. Our jug-eared boy who was growing up thick and stout, I got so I couldn't stand the sight of him either. I started thinking they were both little bastards. And in this way I let the years get away from me.

I wish I could say Shirley and me had words, that one day we just raised hell with each other until we got it all straightened out. But we never did any such thing, not even once during the next almost eighteen years. We raised hell plenty of times about all kinds of different things, but I never let it come up.

There's a world of difference between thinking something and doing it. Like me thinking about shooting Skeeter back in the woods. Jesus is going to ding me for that anyhow, is what Bonnie Maye tells me. Probably so. And there's a world of difference between thinking something and saying it out in the open. And once you say something, you're going to have to do something. I was never sure what I would do. I wasn't sure I cared to know.

So I kept on drinking and laying up at the house and not going to work until the old lady threw me out. Then I stayed up at my brother's and got drunk some more. One day he said to me, didn't I know what Shirley was going through? I never told him anything either. What was I supposed to tell him now? I knew what he meant, though, the whole town talking about us and her having a brand-new baby on top of it all. So I got a little straight and went back home. That's when she cooked one of the fish, took it out of the freezer where it was wrapped up in tinfoil and cooked it whole with butter and a mess of onions. She cooked it too dry, though; all it was was a tough old fish with no flavor to it at all.

There's a sign for you, all right. I look at the old fart. "Why aren't there ever any good signs? You tell me that."

When he opens up his old mouth to speak, I hear these little squeaking sounds way back in his throat like he's got to coax the words up out of there. "A sign is nothing but sign. You make out of it whatever you will."

"What's that owl saying to me, then?"

"He says things got to change. He don't say how; it's all in how you take it."

Mostly what people call love is just another word for pain. Take the old lady's daddy. He made Powell Coal. It was another piddly shit outfit until he engineered that deep shaft. They say you could read about it in some of the books on mining engineering. He had his fine house, his children and grandbabies. One day he stepped into the bathroom and blew his head off. You tell me why.

The old lady will be coming home from the hospital directly. She claims she likes the second shift better, though she's been there long enough to have whatever shift she wants. Time to roust that boyfriend out and get things looking a little respectable around here. When I start to go in, I tell the old fart I'll be seeing him. He gets up with a grunt and starts to move off to his own empty house. "Sleep good," I tell him.

But he doesn't sleep much at all these days, claims he never has. I see his light way back in his kitchen when I'm up in the middle of the night taking a pee. He sits and listens and tells me I ought to do the same.

When the boy is run off, and the gal is upstairs in her bed, I take my last sip of whiskey upstairs and sit myself on the couch still warm from all that wallowing. Now, you take this house, an old company house thrown up with rough sawmill lumber. It wasn't made to last any longer than the mines; the joists are dry-rotting and the floorboards are all warped and crooked, but here it stands. Old worn-out rugs and a TV set on a little wooden table my boy made in his shop class, and the mines gone out ten years ago.

That boy of mine left on out of here for the Air Force. Says not to look for him coming back. I said the same thing myself once; we'll see if he can do better. That gal will be following right behind him when she graduates from school. Nobody but me and Shirley then. I picture her sitting at the kitchen table like she always does on a Sunday morning, looking out over her cup of coffee, and I see whatever goes on in her head is lost to me. Maybe she is like me, looking back at herself and wondering how a gal who had so much spunk came to this sorry place.

I think of Bonnie Maye, still a pretty woman though she has to put the color back in her hair. I think of her sitting up at night giving herself one of her shots in the thigh where the mark won't show. And I think of something else she says, that there's lots of hurtful things coming for us all, things that maybe we're better off not even knowing about. But I listen to the old fart and to the hoot owl out behind the house, and I think otherwise.

Sometimes I think how sheet lightning will come up in a summer's sky and light the night world bright as day. And I think that's what I've been looking for, that's the kind of sign I have been hoping for, the kind that shows you the whole lay of the land, lighting up all your love and wanting and lonesomeness and things past fixing, and things yet to come. Lighting up who you are and can't help but be. If this sign could be given to me, I could put by this liquor and rise up a new man. The same old man, really, but a new man too. A man who holds his heart in his hand for everybody to see and says, "Come on, I'm ready."

If You Meet the Buddha by the Road

The chilly rain was already making Kaye feel trapped and claustrophobic inside her foggy car. Which was the cause, she decided later, of her almost running over a guy riding his bicycle on Brawley School Road. Brawley School Road is narrow and has lots of traffic that time of day when the kids are getting out of school, and here was Kaye, late on the way to picking up Diedra for her dental appointment anyway. She swerved and laid on her horn just to let him know what she thought and drove on. She could have hit him, she was that close and him riding with no light or reflector.

Later on, she would play this scene over and over again to herself. It must have been close to raining sideways when Kaye came up on him hanging on to his racing handlebars and pedaling up a rooster tail, riding his bike right on top of the white line down the side of the highway. And sunglasses, he was riding in sunglasses. She tried to put his picture back together in her head: a white T-shirt, sopping, and those tight black shorts they all wore, his chin and pointy nose aimed straight ahead like he was on a mission, like this was a race for his life or something.

Though she couldn't have seen them, she felt like his bare legs and arms were covered with goose bumps, that he must be riding with hard concentration to get home and jump in the shower. Maybe dark glasses were all he had to protect his eyes. Maybe he was new around here and didn't know how the weather off the lake could sneak up on you. Maybe she should cut him some slack for being so brave and so dumb.

Except it wasn't a stranger at all but Bobby Maclelland, her first ex-husband. She knew as soon as she put together that nose and chin with the rest of the face—cloudy blue eyes and a pinched-up knot of skin between his eyebrows, the part hidden behind his glasses. Whatever sympathy she felt for a wet bicyclist passed. She drove on out to the Brawley Baptist Church, pulled into the parking lot, and waited five minutes to watch him pass just to make sure.

"Why didn't you warn me?" she hollered over the phone at her mom, Nona.

Nona never much liked Bobby Maclelland, but he was a damned sight better than Big Ed Pacoszich, Kaye's second ex-. "Honey, I thought you knew. He's been pedaling that silly bicycle all over town ever since he got back. I saw him pushing a buggy around Harris Teeter doing his grocery shopping in those little black shorts."

"Good God."

"It's no reflection on you. People around here probably lost track of you all even being married. It wasn't that long."

"Oh Momma."

"It's been a while. I'd be more worried about what they're talking around about Ed and his un-huh out at the golf course."

"That's all lies," Kaye told her and hung up. If that story got around, it would be hell on Diedra. She decided it would be better to think about Bobby if only to take her mind off Ed.

It had been sixteen years. Kaye and Bobby got married at the county clerk's office the Saturday after their high school graduation. They were both of age and passed the blood test, what else was there to it? they asked themselves as they drove up to Statesville. The sun shone bright on the furniture outlets and used car lots and three different Get'N'Go stores all advertising two chili dogs for a dollar. "Let's get two after the wedding," Kaye said. "It'll seal our love," Bobby said. Reassuring themselves in this way, they drove on, fully expecting Mrs. Raymond Maclelland, Bobby's mother, to somehow contrive a means of stopping the wedding. Kaye knew they went through with it in part to teach Mrs. Mac a lesson. She couldn't remember when she let herself in on this knowledge. She remembers Nona saying, "Cut off your nose to spite your face," as she was running up a long calico skirt that Kaye would wear with a simple white peasant blouse at the ceremony.

But Mrs. Maclelland did not appear. Instead Lucas Forrest, who smelled of cigar smoke and farts, joined them in matrimony while a couple of their classmates looked on. Then, forgetting the chili dogs, they drove off to the Maclellands' lake lot and threw a party, and camped for a week in the house tent that stayed up all summer on the property.

Every night when a car's lights raked the side of the tent, Kaye held her breath. Surely Mrs. Maclelland knew where they were; surely she intended to do something. Kaye lay awake, fully expecting to be dragged naked from their pinned-together sleeping bags by county deputies. She imagined Lucas had no power to marry them, the marriage was annulled. Or maybe the governor—who was supposedly a very distant relative on Mrs. Maclelland's mother's side—undid it through an executive order based on some ancient law that everybody had forgotten about. Kaye could picture phone calls being made across the state; she saw herself and Bobby on the front page of the Charlotte paper, wrapped in blankets, being pushed into the back of a police cruiser.

Nobody came to the lake lot, no cops; not even their friends came out to see them. Mrs. Mac didn't come. What Kaye had not expected happened. After two weeks in the tent, she and Bobby packed his old Chevy II wagon and drove back to town. Bobby's mother went ahead and let them stay married, let them live in Bobby's bedroom since that was the only place where there was room for them.

Now Kaye thought she wanted to see him. She was sure where he was, right back in his bedroom at Mrs. Maclelland's, 1237 Fieldstone Drive. The National Honor Society certificate was probably still on the green wall, the HeathKit receiver still half-made and spread out on a card table. Mrs. Mac's house was two blocks down and three blocks over from her mother's house. She passed by it all the time, every time she wanted to crawl under the seat of her car.

No, not every time. Sometimes she wanted to take her piece-of-shit VW Rabbit with 130,000 miles on it and crash it right into Mrs. Mac's living room. She could see the corner cabinets buckling, the Blue Willow sliding onto the floor and breaking into pale sandy dust, the pictures of Bobby and his brother Ted getting this honor and that honor and their sainted dad, dead before she ever knew them, all those pictures bursting into hundreds of splintery glass pieces. And Mrs. Mac would get up and help Kaye out of her VW and say, "Why, Kaye, haven't you put on a little weight? I thought so; it looks good on you. It wouldn't on most, but on you—I think it makes you look a little more healthy. How's your little girl? I see you so seldom, I've lost track of her age."

This was a woman the school board was thinking of naming the new elementary school after. Maybe though, like some evil space alien with only limited powers to maintain its human form, Mrs. Maclelland would one day tire herself out. Right on the street in downtown Mooresville, people would see her fangs and claws and slitty eyes. Maybe it would happen in front of Morrow Brothers' and somebody could run right into the hardware department and find an axe or machete or something else big and sharp to take care of her.

Instead, Kaye found herself parked in the drive and saying, "Yes mam, Diedra is fourteen now."

"That's right," Mrs. Mac pretended to remember, "because Bobby went in the service in October and she came along the following May. I don't think we had her at Parkview."

"No, South School." Because Kaye petitioned the school board to let little Diedra go out of her district and Kaye paid the price by having to drop her off and pick her up every day. It was just part of the huge accumulated debt she'd run up in town for ruining Bobby Maclelland's life.

Maybe Bobby's life hadn't been ruined at all. Maybe it was like taking a fish from one aquarium and dumping it in another. That's how much he noticed. That's how come Kaye got hooked on him in the first place. When she moved to town in the sixth grade, Bobby Maclelland was all everybody talked about. Here was this little nearsighted boy who was a genius, who would win a Morehead Scholarship to Carolina, whose biggest problem in life was going to be to decide what good purpose to put all his brains to. God, she hated him going around recess with his hands in his pockets talking big words in his slow, slow voice, not looking at you or anybody else.

It turned out he wasn't a genius at all. "His mother has pushed him and pushed him till she ruined that boy," Nona said. Ted, the older boy, was just regular. He'd done fine in school, was good-looking and quarterbacked the football team. Now he's a lawyer down in Charlotte. When Bobby went into first grade eight years behind him, Mrs. Mac started from Day One saying he was special. What had happened in the meanwhile was that Mr. Raymond Maclelland, manager of the Burlington Textile Mill and the kind of man who saw to it that things got done, like new uniforms for the school band, drove his car into a truckload of Holly Farms chickens. Naturally he was on his way home from another act of civic responsibility, and it made the whole town feel we'd always owe his family something. Everybody started agreeing with Mrs. Mac that Bobby certainly looked to be a wonder.

Kaye was in chemistry with Bobby, though, and she knew. It was almost as hard for him as it was for her. The only difference was that Bobby studied. So she wasn't surprised when he only got to the first interview in the Morehead competition. The way people acted, it seemed like she was the only one who'd figured him out. That's when she fell for him. Everywhere she looked she saw little old Bobby looking lost in the halls, getting back some papers in his classes that read, "B—you can do better than this!" There he sat, over by the window, bleached out in a puddle of light, hair sticking out of his head all crooked and a puny mustache, lost, lost. Then Kaye thought only she could salvage him.

"He's not no prize," Nona told her, but Nona didn't believe in prizes.

"He's sweet."

"I didn't say he wasn't sweet. It's them that fool you, make you feel like you got to be their mommas, and the next thing you know you wind up naked in the back of somebody's car."

"Momma!"

"He's got a momma. That's his biggest problem."

Unlike anybody else Kaye knew, Bobby called his momma Mother. The three of them ate dinner together almost every night for two years, and all Kaye could remember was the sound of long open spaces, a fork knocking against a plate, a glass thumping down on the table, some far-out composition from her music appreciation class: dinnertime in hell. Please pass, may I, thank you, you're quite welcome.

"We always pass the salt and pepper together." Kaye caught herself telling Diedra that just the other night. Oh well, maybe it would be better for her to know such things, maybe it would save her a little grief.

"Bobby is in the garage," Mrs. Mac said. "Why don't you go on in." The garage door waited like a big closed mouth.

Bobby Maclelland sat on a small collapsible stool looking at a bicycle suspended on a repair stand. Maybe there was something to be fixed about the bike, but probably not. Probably he was only admiring it, not because he had put it together just so, but because it simply was. *It is worthy. Its strong thin tubes, its simple structure. The not-quite-parallel construction of the seat tube and the head tube and the gradual bending outward of the narrow fork blades—these are things that hold the eye, contain the eye if you let them.*

He wore a white shirt with the words PUNISH YOUR MACHINE in large blocky black letters on the back. On the front was a brand name for maybe a bicycle company. Kaye had never heard of it; she would have asked him what it was if she thought she could pronounce it correctly. Bobby seemed to have more muscles in his arms, though his chest was still narrow and he seemed to be a little bent. She could see him as an old man, the kind of old man who goes away to a cabin in the mountains and spends the rest of his life reading the same three books over and over. And he had a pierced ear with a tiny gold ring in it and a wispy, almost invisible goatee.

Kaye felt weird, the same way you feel when you go see somebody in the hospital. "Hey," she said, "long time, no see."

"I guess I've been busy," he said. And she wondered if he meant all the times he'd been back to Mooresville on leave and she'd steered clear of Fieldstone Drive, or the more than a month she guessed he'd been back in town this time. Or if he meant instead that he had circled the world, that he had been to Tokyo, to Rome, to all those places that sounded so rich bouncing off the inside of your head, while she and Ed Pacoszich, Mrs. Mac, and Nona had been caught in some kind of suspended animation and had not gone anywhere at all.

"I guess you're out of the Air Force."

He said he'd been out for some time. And he told her about his life in Alaska where he'd worked as a commercial fisherman, in the West where he'd herded sheep with old men who could hardly speak English, and in lots of other places where he just took odd jobs. Painting houses and being a night watchman, those were the best. When he talked, his voice would sometimes stop and his lips keep moving while his eyes roamed around the room as if remembering at all had become a struggle.

"I bet you saved some money." Money worried Kaye, but she hadn't meant to let it out.

"Yeah," he admitted, he had, and he'd used some of it to travel. But now he thought he'd be staying in Mooresville a while. Now he thought he knew what he wanted to do. Kaye waited, thinking how easy it was to believe he really was a genius. Part of the way you got to be a genius was to be confused and misunderstood for a long time until one day you just scratched out some equations on a chalk board and everybody saw it. "There's just a smidgen of difference between a real genius and a crazy person," Nona always said. You might get this idea in your head and just not be able to spit it out, it would knock around in there like a fly against a window until it wore itself out, until you wore yourself out thinking about it.

Bobby might be getting ready to cure cancer right in his mother's garage. He said, "I think I want to build bicycle frames."

You could buy bikes at Kmart all day long for eighty-nine dollars and they'd put them together for you. Kaye had bought a fifteen-speed for Diedra. And Bobby wanted to make just the frame part and sell it for maybe eight or nine hundred or a thousand dollars. He thought when he got going good he could build three or four a month. "You'll never make any money that way," Kaye told him.

Then she said, "You're crazy," and felt a little wind of relief blow over her. She had done right; leaving Bobby Maclelland had not been the biggest mistake of her life.

The whole thing made her mad. Pulling out, she made a point of running over the corner of the yard beside the driveway; Mrs. Maclelland hated that. Stuck between Bobby and Mrs. Mac, Kaye was feeling right now exactly how she had felt when she was married.

Mrs. Mac always sat at the head of the dinner table, talking like she had all the answers, "This abortion decision, what do you think of that?" It was in the paper; Kaye read the Supreme Court had made abortion legal. Bobby looked down into his plate. For all Kaye knew he was still stuck on a calculus problem.

She had worried enough about getting pregnant; Nona told her she better not if she knew what was good for her. "I think it'll save us all a lot of trouble," Kaye told Mrs. Mac. What had she meant by that? Because when the time came, when she found herself pregnant and Bobby not even the father and her in the middle of the semester, the thought of getting rid of the baby never crossed her mind. Ed Pacoszich was the daddy.

Big Ed Pacoszich. That's what everybody in Mooresville still calls him. Only you want to make your voice low and rough when you say it. "Hey, Big Ed." Even women will do it, dropping down into their lowest contralto and warbling a little to let him know they're teasing, "Hellooo, Big Ed." You got to love him, seeing his real estate ads in the paper. There's Ed up in the corner with his glasses cocked real funny up on his nose because the temple pieces are too short and there's his quote of the week: "When somebody says, 'Any idiot can run this joint,' that's a plus as far as I'm concerned, because sooner or later any idiot probably will." Then come the listings for houses and lake lots.

For a while Big Ed got to be rich. IBM came into Charlotte and all of a sudden families who'd had property out on the lake were being offered twenty, thirty times what they paid for it. Ed took care of the business and bought himself a Lincoln Town Car. Most of these were weekend places, some with an old travel trailer pulled out on them and set on blocks, some with just a picnic table as a sign they were owned. The kinds of places where Bobby Maclelland and Kaye spent their honeymoon. Mrs. Mac sold her lot for a good price, but she didn't let Ed handle the transaction. It didn't matter; just then he had more than he could manage.

By then, nobody was surprised about Ed. By then he had shown us all. There are four Pacoszich boys in all and Ed is the baby. The rest are built like their mom, a little woman, personality like a spitz dog. Mean boys. They played on the end and in the defensive backfield and could put a hurt on boys twice their size. Then here came Ed, big and slow and with a glass eye from some monkey business when he was little. What it was, the others made him run while they lit and threw firecrackers behind him, only one of the crackers got out ahead of him. He wound up playing tackle. Nona said anybody who could manage to survive to adulthood in that household would have to have a little gumption.

Nona said this when Bobby and Kaye were riding to UNC at Charlotte every day with Ed. When it caught everybody by surprise that Ed was even going to college. It was just UNC-C despite what Mrs. Mac said about it being an up-and-coming institution, but the rest of the Pacoszich boys worked as carpenters and most thought Ed would do the same. Nona wouldn't be able to find another good thing to say about Ed for years once Kaye and he started messing around.

"Bobby Mac's your *husband*," she told Kaye when she finally got her to admit what everybody in town already was saying.

"Oh, Momma, don't. Bobby's sweet and all, and I know this is going to hurt him, but I'm in love with Ed."

"Luuve! Luuve!" Nona moaned like a shot dove. "You made a choice, girl, now you better stick by it." Kaye thought of her own dad, who'd worked his whole life as a telephone lineman and came home every evening to fall asleep behind the paper. He was in the living room sleeping right then. What did Nona think she meant when she said, "Bobby's a good boy"?

"I can't help it," Kaye told her and wouldn't say anything else. In fact, she had been screwing around with Ed on a fold-out lounge chair in the back of his truck at a drive-in movie when she got herself knocked up.

"It's just hormones," Nona said.

Kaye hadn't thought Nona knew what hormones were. She was wrong about that too. Had she loved Ed? Had she loved Bobby? Was it all because the Chevy II threw a rod? Mrs. Mac or maybe Ted would have bought them a new car, but Bobby wouldn't ask. He was stubborn and proud and expected Kaye to be too. They helped with the gas and rode in with Ed. Every morning, they went to Charlotte the back way down Coddle Creek Road, riding three to the seat, squashed in together but too sleepy to care. Bobby was majoring in something hard—chemical engineering, electrical engineering. He was always in labs; he was always having to stay late and study. Kaye majored in psychology, and she wasn't sure what Ed finally majored in.

At first, they'd wait for Bobby at the Sonic and have hamburgers and Cokes, do their homework in a booth and talk. Ed said, "What'd the tie say to the hat?" Kaye didn't know. "You go on ahead, and I'll hang around. Haw, haw."

That was Ed. Always something like that, some crazy something. Gradually they moved on down to Gus's 49er, the bar where everybody hung out on Fridays. It was pretty empty the rest of the time. They'd get a pitcher of beer with their burgers and split it. "Hey, I'd rather have a bottle in front of me than a frontal lobotomy," Ed told her.

He taught Diedra these one-liners as a little girl, and he'd coax them out of her for company. "Lo-bo-to-my," she piped, proudly finishing up the line. It seems like that was all there was to their marriage, a pretty little girl who said funny things, Ed off making a deal. He started in selling shoes at Shoe Show, that discount place out on the bypass, and somehow finagled himself into real estate. Nona said a few good things then. She admitted Ed was a good provider; she laughed at his jokes. "Nona!" He'd be calling her from work to check on Diedra. "Why did the Polack wear a black rubber? Think about it, think. I'll tell you later."

Kaye had left him. She caught him screwing around with one of the lady realtors. But she felt like she was on the verge of screwing around herself. Just a feeling, a kind of sparky edge she got around certain men. Maybe she wasn't even sure what it meant. She knew now, though; these days none of the men were sparking back.

Of course Big Ed knew Bobby was back in town. Knowing pretty much everything that goes on in Mooresville is his business. How else can you get rich selling real estate? He had seen Bobby riding his bicycle here and around, out by the lake, over towards Concord, even way down the old back roads on the way to Charlotte.

It didn't surprise him. People say Mooresville took on a cross-country running team because of Bobby Mac, that his mother wanted some sport he could play to impress the Morehead Committee and the school board put it in and got an English teacher to coach it. What nobody expected was for Bobby Maclelland to be pretty good at it, pretty good for a three-A school runner. You could see him out after school running in the pouring rain, running all through the winter in nothing but short pants.

After the Chevy II broke, Ed and Kaye would stop on the way home from UNC-C and let him off to run the rest of the way—five or six miles, sometimes ten or fifteen. They'd play a game guessing where Bobby must be on his run: at the house with the Oldsmobile full of cord wood, at Mackie's welding shop, at the mailbox with the cardinals painted on it. Finally, Bobby fell out of their conversation. But never out of Ed's imagination. Even when he started screwing around with Kaye, he pictured Bobby the way he saw him out of his rearview mirror, a guy growing smaller, sometimes just a speck on a hilltop, but still running, his arms and legs red from the cold, his head cocked to one side, some dried-up spit on his cheek.

Now that he'd done it a few times, Ed thought you must have to look down on a man to start fucking his wife, or maybe look down on the wife. Either way, it never turned out so good. They'd start out testing the mattress in one of his rental units, move on to getting drunk and running all over the county hiding from her old man. End up fighting. He knew it was over when he started buying chewing tobacco.

That's not what happened with him and Kaye. They were younger; maybe it was hormones and too much beer. He thought of his brothers, their capable delivery of violence from the defensive backfield. It wasn't true that he'd played in the line because of his eye; it was safer there. You didn't have to throw yourself through space, inflicting pain, welcoming pain in return. Bobby Mac knew something about pain too, Ed saw. Bobby's pain was more private, probably too serious, but it was worth respecting.

He thought he ought to drive over and see Bobby, talk to him about a condo that was opening up down on the lake. Maybe they'd have a beer together sometime or go to a ball game. Let bygones be.

The only other full-grown man who rides a bike around here is Pedaling Pete. You can count on him for some yard work if you stay right on him, otherwise he's sure to foul it up, cut your hedges right down to the ground, pull up your flowers and leave the weeds. It's hard to guess how much he does know — enough to get around town on his old green bike with a big old basket on the handlebars and a milk crate on the rack behind. Full of tools, full of junk he'll stop and pick up in the street.

In the summer he'll be over at the pool all afternoon sitting in the bleachers they have for the mommas to look out for their kids just in case the lifeguards don't. It's hard not to feel sorry for him looking at those high school girls in their bathing suits and him probably feeling as horny as any ordinary guy but not having the sense to do anything about it. It's hard not to get the willies too. Somehow the cops and the lifeguards know when to run Pete off before something is said, before a boyfriend or a brother decides he has to do something.

Nona thought about Pete and about Bobby. She thought about them each riding their bikes here and there — imagining their routes in little dotted lines crisscrossing but them never meeting up. Who would she feel most sorry for?

That would surprise Kaye if she heard it, Nona feeling sorry for Bobby Mac. "A dreamy boy like that never amounts to a thing. Mark me," Nona told her. "He won't get you a pot to piss in."

When it was over, Kaye thought her momma was right. Bobby could sit and think longer than anybody she ever saw. Thinking about what? "Oh nothing," he'd say.

"Come on, what?"

"Nothing."

"What! Bobby, dammit."

Do you see depth in the mirror because you taught yourself to see it there? Depth in the mirror must be an illusion since it's just a flat surface. We believe the world has depth, therefore the reflected world has depth too?

Kaye would have to holler and start pummeling him on the chest and arms. That would get him moving. But she saw. Bobby Maclelland could spend his life in his father's old Barcalounger and never guess he was missing a thing.

The next time Kaye went to see Bobby, she took along Diedra and her bike. She took the bike since maybe fixing it would make Bobby feel like he was doing something useful. She wasn't sure why she took Diedra. "You ought to meet my first old boyfriend," she told her and thought this fib was really closer to the truth than what had really happened. Bobby *was* a boy then and he really had been a friend, too. Whatever he was, it doesn't seem now like he ever had been what she'd call a lover or a husband.

Nobody was around at the Maclellands', so Kaye let herself in. "Momma!" Diedra said. She was scared of Mrs. Mac, too. But it was only the garage.

The pieces of bicycles Bobby had ordered were here, flimsy boxes of bluish tubes. They could be a bicycle; they could be any old thing. And to hold them together, the joints looked as rough as old lead water pipes. Bobby had made a work bench out of sawhorses and boards, and had made a pegboard for his few tools. The whole thing looked desperate, fly-by-night.

In the middle of the bench was a small spiral notebook, the eighty-nine-cent kind, open, with a pen still across the page. *The radial spoke wheel is not only mechanically unreliable, but aesthetically too simple to please the eye. The four-cross has an angle more acute, a more pleasing play of relationships near the hub. Yet even for touring, I think it's too soft, too springy. Why is it that what strikes the eye as more beautiful cannot be equally functional? Consider: the chambered nautilus. The beehive. What about these?*

Good Lord, thought Kaye. She moved away before Diedra caught her reading the notebook. She looked around the garage, and it dawned on her that Bobby was living in this garage. A bivouac hammock hung from the ceiling by two stout hooks; a grass mat lay on the floor, and next to it Bobby had lined up his shoes—flip-flops, heavy hiking shoes, three pairs of worn-out running shoes and a newer looking pair. A cardboard box held his clothes, all the clothes Kaye could see, and some other boxes turned on their sides made shelves for his books. Fat books, the kinds of books that professors used to take for granted you'd read, or expected that you'd want to run right out and read as soon as possible. Lots of paper markers stuck out the tops of all of them.

Kaye snuck a look at Diedra, busy fooling with the bike tubes and lugs, and flipped the notebook back a few pages. *Two things have made Western Civilization worthwhile: the bicycle and the pocket knife. Otherwise, it's all been a waste of effort.* The full pages were made brittle by Bobby's tiny writing, pressed hard into the paper. No dates. The edges were beat-up and dog-eared. Kaye bet Bobby had owned this notebook a long time. She wanted to take it home where she could read it in peace, to find out what Bobby Mac really thought, to find out what he might have said about her.

It's easy to sneak up on people on a bicycle even when you're not thinking about sneaking.

Kaye's car was in the drive; pulling up the garage door could surprise only her. But this was probably the first time Bobby Mac had seen Diedra to know who she was, so maybe he surprised himself too. She was Ed Pacoszich's kid, there was no doubt about that. It's a shame she was going through a self-conscious phase, taller than Kaye and already stooping a little with her arms wrapped around her chest. Ed's nose too; it hadn't looked so bad on him, Kaye thought.

Bobby clomped over to his work bench and closed the notebook; then he offered them some water out of his ice chest. Seeing him maneuver around the garage in his bicycling shoes, Kaye thought of some futuristic man who had evolved past ordinary walking, who'd found some other means of making his way. "Sit down," he said, forgetting there was only the camp stool. Brought back to earth, he could only be a clumsy misfit.

"I don't get it," Kaye said, "what's wrong with the house? What's wrong with your room?"

"Oh. It's Mother's house."

Nobody would argue with that.

There are teachers you might remember fondly for a while after they taught you, the nice ones who had treats for Christmas and read aloud after recess while you rested your head on your desk. After a while, though, time with such teachers gets blurred like the waking-up time just after a nap. The memory of the sixth grade with Mrs. Mac would remain. She was a teacher who knew everything, such as when you did not have a pencil. And there would be hell to pay for not having a pencil, for not having it sharpened and ready. Not the hell of the mythical paddle in the principal's office but the hell of grinding humiliation as you walked to the front of the class and gave Mrs. Mac a nickel and she gave you a new blue pencil that said Burlington Mills. The hell of standing before a sentence chalked up on the board and stuttering between "lie" and "lay." The regular school life of passing notes, gazing out the window, and hiding gum or a booger on the underside of a desk was suspended in her room. Slowly, she bent children in the direction of order, of civilized human behavior. The older Pacoszich boys are good examples of her influence. Showing up on time with the right tools— they'll tell you that's the key to getting any job done.

More folks should get up early enough to see Mrs. Mac in her powder-blue robe walking out to the end of the drive to get the Charlotte paper. With her hair stringing down and makeup off, you could see what it cost her to manufacture such concentrated righteous power. And you could see Mrs. Raymond Maclelland is a much shorter woman than you probably remembered.

Kaye's Diedra was taller than Mrs. Mac. Kaye herself was a little taller, but somehow it didn't matter. Being in her house was still a shrinking drain. "I'll bet your mom is glad you're back," she told Bobby.

He said he guessed she was.

Kaye said, "I'll bet she's hoping you'll finish your degree."

"Yeah, Mother's expectations and mine are a little different." That was it, the way the Maclellands talked. They just said things and went on and did them, expecting whatever they said to come true.

Kaye knew better. Talk was wind blowing against a rock. You could talk till the cows came home, as Nona would say. There was Kaye's daddy on the couch who had not painted the living room in twenty years of talking about it even though painting was something he was good at. Nona was the same way, always going to write a letter to the paper. So was Kaye. And Diedra? Sometimes Kaye wondered what would have happened if she'd lied and said Diedra was Bobby's baby. Her child would have grown up surrounded by educational toys and would have had all the right books read to her. Would it have made any difference?

Bobby was showing Diedra how the lugs and tubes would go together to make a bike. He picked up a smooth shiny lug that had been filed and finished and slid it on the tube like a little collar.

"Three hours of work there," he said. It turned out Bobby disliked the noise of power tools and planned to do most of the work by hand.

Here was yet another crazy thing. "Why don't you just pound them down with rocks?" Kaye said.

Diedra looked at her mom crossly, and when Bobby offered her one of the rough lugs and a file she took it and began awkwardly to wear away the rough metal. "You can't mess up," he told her and offered a lug and file to Kaye as well. She wouldn't take it.

"So how is Ed?" Bobby asked as he shaped his own lug. Kaye had taken the camp stool and Diedra sat on the floor Indian style working away—and taking everything in, of course. "Mother wrote me that you all had broken up. I wondered." He filed along. "I can't tell you how often you both have been in my thoughts."

Kaye saw this was the whole trouble with Bobby Maclelland. He could say these things and mean them, mean that he probably still really cared though he had no good reason to, and yet at the very same time by saying them show how much he lacked good sense.

———————

Listen, Ed will tell you, most of the real estate biz is style. He was in the habit of carrying a matching gold pen-and-pencil set. He thought it made the right impression when he whipped one out to doodle some figures on an envelope for a prospective buyer. Ed thought he took to style naturally; he knew that if you ran your Lincoln through the car wash every morning, had that gold ballpoint and calf-skin briefcase, it was that much easier for people to see the world as rich in things and to feel sore at themselves for having to do without. They wouldn't be able to take it; they'd buy. Whether thanks to Mrs. Mac's influence or not, he believed in education and went to every sales-improvement seminar he could.

Still, some things couldn't be helped. He had always perspired heavily and lately had put on weight. His pants were tight through the thighs, his shirts tight through the shoulders. It was getting harder to keep all his belly inside his belt. IBM was laying some people off, sending some others back up north. Ed knew this and so did his realtor buddies; so did the guys who ran the seminars. Right now nobody was buying.

There was the business out at the golf course, too. Here's the way Nona heard it. Poor Mrs. Gertrude Tabor, coming into town for a meeting of the United Methodist Women, saw Ed standing outside the windbreak where the course runs along the 150 bypass. At first she thought he had just snuck behind the trees there to take a pee. Maybe, she thought, he was only thinking about whether the ones playing golf could see him and not the ones in their cars. "Don't make much sense," said

Nona, "but that's Ed. Except the way he was holding it? Kind of waving it around? Made her think elsewise."

"Momma," Kaye told her, "I can't help what Ed does."

"I know. Except you might want to watch him around Diedra."

Ed wouldn't do anything to Diedra, Kaye felt sure of that. At such times, though, she wanted to sit down on her mother's couch and bawl. Here she was, a thirty-four-year-old woman whose life had just run off the tracks.

Nona had three kids. The oldest, a girl, was a lady disk jockey in Asheville where she was famous and loved and had her picture on a billboard. And she had a boy who was in computers and who had kids of his own. Happy kids who ran around the house dueling with foam rubber swords. It wasn't Nona's fault, Kaye knew that. Even though Nona was a heavy woman, she was always busy. When she wasn't cooking or doing the wash or making up her husband's lunch bucket, she was crocheting another afghan or some slippers. Kaye grew up and left Nona's house feeling independent and smart.

She had been the cheerleader with spunk. When Mooresville was ahead 40–0, when the adults and kids in the bleachers lost track of the game and turned to gossiping, she was down on the sidelines hollering through her megaphone, "Come on, yell!" It wasn't that she expected life to be as simple as a ball game; she knew better than that. But in those days she had had a clarity of purpose, and it hadn't mattered what the next new thing would be. When it came along, she would meet it head-on.

Nowadays when they did something together, Diedra trailed her as if she were a kite fighting to get off its string. In the car, she leaned sourly against the passenger side door willing herself to turn invisible. Like any kid that age, she had an instinctive knowledge of what her mother would hate. Diedra started hanging around at Bobby Mac's garage workshop, filing lugs, watching him build his jigs, listening to him talk. Because there in his own place he would just blurt whatever came into his head, and Diedra picked it all up.

"Momma, there's a goose in a bottle. How do you get it out?"

Kaye was trying to balance her checkbook. She avoided it for weeks on end, so when she did do it there was an element of panicked suspense involved. "I don't know, honey, you tell me."

"Come on, Momma, a goose in a bottle. Think about it."

"I can't right now."

But Diedra went right on. It was some rigmarole about getting to be a Buddhist monk and how they asked you the answer to this riddle and if you didn't know it, they hit you with a bamboo stick until finally one day you just got it and they didn't hit you anymore.

"Honey, think: did we eat at The Dixie Pig last Wednesday after I got you at Momma's? I need to find this missing check. Or at least guess how much it might have been."

"It's out," Diedra said.

"What?"

"It's out. You get it out by just saying it's out. Get it?"

"Did Big Ed tell you that?"

"Bobby Maclelland."

"I thought it was a little deep for Ed." But where had they eaten? Kaye tried to reconstruct the day, beginning with dropping Diedra off at school, thinking how easy it would be to just say, "It's paid," and any check she wrote would be covered.

Big Ed and Bobby showed up together at the ball game Friday night. The team's not so hot, not like when the Pacoszich boys played, and you would see the cars lining up at six o'clock to get into an eight o'clock game. Ed still likes to go, likes to work the crowd, to find out who's new in town, who might be looking to buy or sell. People were standoffish. Maybe it was Bobby Mac; he had a way of making anybody nervous, standing around and looking everything over, never looking you in the face. He'd be humming a song and you were never sure he heard a word you said. Ed tried to think so, but he knew it wasn't Bobby Mac. It was what everybody heard about him out at the Elks' Club golf course.

"Hell, let's just sit up on the top bleacher where we can see better," he told Bobby Mac. Up with the mill hands and the guys who sipped out of bottles in paper bags, up where they hollered down advice and insults to the coaches and refs.

"Listen," Big Ed said after a while—the other team, West Iredell for God's sake, was moving the ball steadily down the field. It pained Ed. "You need to get yourself fixed up with a shop."

"How come?" Bobby Mac said. He was spacey, he thought Ed meant a little store.

"No, a workshop, a factory so when your business takes off you'll have the room. Price's Gulf station is up for sale. You couldn't make it a gas station anymore, not downtown. But it's got two service bays, lots of 220 outlets. Comes with the grease rack, compressors, lots of good shit."

Bobby Mac cranked up his rusty voice. Big Ed remembered from riding in the truck; Bobby was no talker. "Most people think they want a bicycle with 72- or 73-degree angles. I myself have a bicycle with 73-degree angles and a fully wrapped seat-stay."

"No kidding," said Ed.

"They don't understand steep angles are no good for touring. My bicycles won't be for everybody, they'll be for people who understand."

"Yeah." Ed screwed up his good eye to Bobby and ignored the away team's final push into the end zone.

"They'll have 68-, 69-degree angles, longer fork rakes."

"Once that catches on, though," Ed told him. He pictured a sign, maybe a billboard as you came into town right along with the welcomes from Burlington Mills, Jaycees, and Rotary that would tell the world this was the home of Bobby Maclelland's famous homemade bicycles. "I may have to buy one myself. Put me down for one."

"You wouldn't want one, Ed."

Final score Mooresville 0, West Iredell 28. Bobby Mac was the damnedest person. You tried to talk him up, and he talked himself down just as fast. Who ever heard of getting into the business of making a product nobody wanted? Still, Ed told him he wanted to buy one of his bikes even though it looked like he would have to go over to Bobby's place and have himself measured for it. Everything Bobby planned to do was custom, which appealed to Ed. He'd never had a custom any-thing in his life unless you counted his glass eye.

———————

"I don't want Diedra over at Bobby Maclelland's house," Kaye told Ed. "I'm telling you so she won't be there when she's supposed to be with you."

"Why not? It keeps her off the street." They both knew Diedra hadn't been on the street, she had been curled up on Nona's couch every afternoon. Still, there was something about Bobby Mac. "Hey, you think he'll seduce her with his brain power just like he did her mom?"

"You shut up, Ed. Bobby's nice, I just don't want her over there."

"OK, he's kind of crazy. But you can't hold that against him," Ed told her. "Listen, a guy has a flat tire outside an insane asylum . . ."

Kaye said, "You told me that joke in the Sonic, way back when. 'I may be crazy but I'm not stupid.' Remember?" Maybe that's it, maybe crazy or stupid is the only option. Maybe stupid was better. Kaye thought of the other Pacoszich boys leaning against the sides of their shiny fixed-up cars, spitting tobacco juice and talking about the ball game. Maybe they were the only people she knew who had good sense. Pounding nails all day, they thought about pounding nails.

"It all goes to show he's no crazier than we are," Ed told her.

Kaye could have said something about the golf course if she'd wanted to, but it would only make things harder. Here was Diedra, a shy child, smart—being smart only made it worse—getting ready to wander off into drugs or devil worship or whatever the new fad was. Kaye could feel it.

As if to prove her right, the very next afternoon Diedra did not ride her bike over to Nona's but went to Bobby Mac's instead. Poor Nona, crocheting in front of the TV set halfway in a trance, didn't catch what Kaye was talking about until she was out the door again. "Let her be," Nona said, thinking there was a world of difference between a silly boy and a silly man. Anybody who went around the grocery store bumping his cart into you or the piled-up displays, stuffing his groceries into a grimy backpack at the checkout, had got past any kind of woman hungriness Diedra needed to be afraid of.

Kaye pulled in the Maclellands' driveway and laid on the horn. "A horn," Mrs. Mac used to tell Big Ed every morning when he came to pick them up for college, "is to be used as a warning, not a summons." Kaye wanted Diedra to know it could be both.

Maybe it was good that Bobby came out with her and helped load her bike on the rack clamped on Kaye's bumper. "That kind of rack," Bobby said through a yawn coming up in his voice, "gets your tires hot. Sometimes they blow."

"Good," Kaye said and backed out over the corner of Mrs. Mac's lawn.

Bobby was getting away with this. He was sitting in that garage every afternoon fiddling around with his joints and tubes and what-have-you, without a care in the world. Kaye had plenty of cares for both of them in case he wondered—which he did not. Or maybe he did. Maybe he worried like hell that Kaye was between jobs, watching her unemployment checks wind down, waiting for her credit cards to start maxing out. His Bobby Mac spaciness made him forget to ask; one day he would blurt it out, probably to Diedra.

There had been plenty of other times when she blamed him for her pain. Nights when she sat at home with Diedra while Big Ed was out showing a house, or stopping off at some joint to shoot a game of pool afterwards. Then Kaye pictured Bobby on some Pacific island sweating in a hut with a rifle on his lap guarding a dark mysterious airplane. Or in a white dome in Greenland wading out in the snow once a day to read a thermometer. She imagined his ill will and misery beamed up to a passing satellite and down onto her. With a cranky baby in a rental apartment with a bath and no shower, Kaye found some comfort thinking Bobby was behind it.

Except now she saw him as just the first of a series of wrong choices. Bobby. Ed. A useless college degree. She had worked hard to get it, too, leaving Diedra with Nona sometimes for days at a time, driving home some nights so tired she saw things in the road, a cactus waving its limbs, a camel. Only to find out all she could do was work as a receptionist at a dentist's office, a school secretary, an ad saleswoman for the local weekly. Nothing jobs, she'd quit them all until this last one, working in the office at a construction company. That one just ended when the building was up. Hey, Ed said, she could get her license and sell just like him. Right, Kaye thought. She knew. She had lost her spunk.

As they rode along through a Mooresville of flat brick houses, blue and beige cars, of niceness you could cut with a knife, Diedra said, "Mom? You know Benito Mussolini? The Italian dictator?" Kaye could tell that Diedra didn't think she knew who Mussolini was.

"Yeah, honey. They strung him up upside down." Kaye could still see the picture in her world history book. Was that right? Could Diedra be seeing such things in her schoolbooks?

"Oh. Well, he thought everybody in Italy ought to eat a banana every day."

"So?"

"So Bobby says that's the way to human happiness, potassium. And he says it goes to show that even a creep can sometimes have a good idea."

"Potassium. Well God bless Bobby if that's all it takes."

"It doesn't. It's more complicated than that."

"OK, what else does it take?"

"Bobby says it takes love."

If Kaye had not been trying to shift gears and go around a corner at the same time she might have slapped her daughter. Instead she drove on and did not let herself say what she thought. What did Diedra know? She was a child.

Pedaling Pete came up beside them at a stoplight. Pete always obeyed the law. He had a grass rake tied to the frame of his bicycle so its tines fanned out behind his wheel like some kind of tail. Kaye looked into his face, maybe for the first time since she had been Diedra's age and she stared back at Pete staring at her at the pool. He had a broad forehead and blue eyes, but except for a certain jowliness, his face was empty, peaceful.

As they pulled away, Diedra said, "Bobby says Pete is his alter ego."

"Oh shut up," Kaye told her.

"He says Pete's got the heart of a fifteen-year-old. We'd all live to be a hundred if we did like Pedaling Pete."

There are lots of things Bobby said that Diedra never told her momma. Killing the Buddha for example. If you meet the Buddha on the road, you're supposed to kill him because anybody who claims to be the Buddha can't be. What this meant, Diedra wasn't sure. Kaye had never taken her to church. Nona took her around to the Baptist church on South Main for a while, dumped her off for Sunday school, and came back at eleven to pick her up. Diedra would come out of the building and find Nona in her old Falcon parked as far away from the church as you could be and still be in the parking lot. Nona, in her bathrobe and crocheted slippers, would be reading the funny papers.

Every Sunday Diedra cried. Not because people were mean. There was usually Kool-Aid and a cookie or a candy bar cut up in tiny bits to illustrate the parable of the loaves and fishes. People were nice, but their niceness was all a part of belonging in the same way Jesus, Joseph, and Mary belonged and Nona, Kaye, and Diedra did not. Ed had already started wandering off, coming home late on Saturday nights or not coming home at all.

Diedra told Ed the riddle about the goose in the bottle. She could tell Ed anything; if it wasn't a joke, he just forgot it. "Pretty good," he said. "Tell Bobby this one when you see him: If you're Australian in the kitchen and Asian in the bedroom, what are you in the bathroom?"

She looked at him sideways.

"Come on," Ed said. But when she just sat there, he said, "European."

"That joke's old as you are," she told him, and she thought, it wasn't the same thing at all.

Descending Egg Rock Hill by moonlight: As speed gathers and with no real light, the ground seems to fall away. I could have been going a hundred,

I could have been motionless. I felt like I was leaving the earth, leaving myself.

The next evening after she made sure Diedra was with Nona, Kaye went over to Bobby Maclelland's. The air was chilly and it was starting to get dark early, but the garage door was open and Bobby was bent over his work table. It was different now. The table was heavy wood and in the middle was a huge iron plate with funny-shaped steel rods coming out of it. And stretched across those rods was something that now was looking like a bicycle. Anybody could tell it was starting to be a bicycle.

Whatever Bobby was doing, welding or soldering or whatever, was tedious and he had on funny safety glasses with shields down the sides. He didn't look up. The thing about Bobby, anyhow, was that you couldn't tell whether he knew you were there and just couldn't be bothered, or whether he didn't have a clue. Kaye sat on the camp stool and watched him. Then she pulled the stool around so it would be in his line of sight.

"Have you thought much about what it means for something to be straight? I mean, the concept is easy enough. But really straight? To make something straight?" He said this without seeming to look up, without letting her know he'd seen her.

"It matters, huh?"

"Misaligned and it's not worth a damn."

"Maybe Diedra's coming over here bothering you, messing up your concentration."

"Diedra's a good kid."

"Bobby, I don't want Diedra coming around here."

"She's a good kid. She takes an interest. She wants to know what's what."

That was the problem right there. What, exactly, *was* what in Bobby Mac's mind? And Diedra just now was so impressionable. "I don't want her over here," Kaye said.

Bobby started turning off his equipment, moving around his work table putting things up, pulling off his funny glasses. Of course, he wouldn't let himself look at her. "What do you think we do? We talk. I try to keep her entertained." She looked at his face, pale and hollow.

She'd seen it this way before. When they were high school kids, when she started thinking Nona was right, that she ought to break up with Bobby and look for somebody with more common sense. He would get on some kick about the Student Council showing movies after school and sending the money to Bangladesh. And because he was Bobby Mac, he went straight into the meeting and wasted everybody's time telling them this was what they should do. Then he got mad when nobody listened.

Every time she got to thinking she couldn't hurt him, that nobody could hurt him, that you might have to holler to get his attention, it happened. There he would be just like he was now, sitting across the room, his face going red, his jaw trembling like at any minute he might howl. Maybe, Kaye thought, he was hurting all the time.

It would be hard to say. You could go by Mrs. Mac's any time of day or night and the garage door was liable to be up and Bobby in there working away. You might see him riding his bike any time too. Didn't he rest? Go to the movies? To church or the bowling alley? Didn't he do anything like regular people?

When brazing a fitting, you should think about brazing a fitting; when cutting a tube, you should think about cutting a tube. This is the virtue of work.

Bobby Mac told Diedra about his rides. He told her about riding at dawn and in the middle of the night, too. She started to picture him everywhere along the road as she traveled to and from school, to the store with her mother. She saw him on these roads, pedaling fast, up hills and down, swirling leaves behind him as he went around curves. And she saw him on other roads too. Bobby Mac was a speck on the winding dirt road to Alaska. He might be passing people pulling their belongings behind an ox in Thailand or riding against a wall of volcanic rock in Hawaii. Every picture of every place in Nona's *National Geographic*s was a place Bobby Mac could have been on his bicycle. He'd been everywhere; he told her so, to places you could never even get to in a car. Where you can't ride, you can carry it. He had thrown his bike up on a bus and taken it on ferryboats.

"How did you know you could do things on your bike?"

"Oh I just wanted to go places when I was in the Air Force and didn't have a car." When he was busy like he was now, tapping a bottom bracket, you just had to sit and wait until he got all the words out. "I was stuck on base and I felt like there was a whole world to see that was just out there. . . ." He stopped and wiped his hands on the little apron he wore. Diedra could tell he was seeing all this in his head. With Bobby Mac it was like what he was thinking about might just take him over, he might forget you were around, or forget to talk out loud.

"Yeah?"

"This was Texas . . . hill country. It's not like there were specific things to go see. Everything was there to see, and it didn't matter if other people had seen it before, I had to see it for myself. Get it?"

"Why?"

When he looked up from his work this time, he looked like he had been caught cheating off somebody's test paper. "I can't tell you that."

"Oh, come on."

"No, I can't." He went on biting the tap into the steel. "Well, I guess I was sick of myself. I wanted to fill myself up with everything else, everything that wasn't me. And that's the only way I could think of."

Probably Bobby Mac thought Diedra was a pretty good kid because she didn't press him too much; he got antsy when people pressed. It was just vertigo. His talk was a scary carnival ride, and she couldn't take too much of it.

But at night when she couldn't sleep, Diedra saw herself setting out on her bicycle. Everything she would need would fit in her backpack, and she would sleep in the woods or in the spare bedrooms of people who would take her in just to hear about her adventures. What would those adventures be? So far she couldn't say except they would *not* be Mooresville, not the same old ride from Nona's to Sloop's grocery store to the swimming pool and home to Kaye. There would be rainy days, of course, and mountains, and trucks. Bobby Mac said trucks made their own vacuum and sometimes he worried they could pass too close and pull a cyclist down. She would be ready for all that, and ready for something she was so far not able to imagine to be waiting for her around some curve, at the top of some long hill.

Such stuff would have surprised Kaye only in the way it was so much like her own thoughts when she was Diedra's age. She got mad at herself when she considered how it'd all turned out. One day Bobby Mac had pushed his bike to the main gate of Bergstrom AFB, signed out, and set out to lap the world with nothing to guide him but an old gas station map. On that day she was probably carrying a baby on her hip around the UNC-C library, trying to find some articles and getting dirty looks from everybody. In some way their brains had been switched, a mad scientist had stuck their heads in big aluminum cocoons, hooked up some wires, and pulled a switch. Suddenly, Bobby Mac was out in the world, and Kaye was sitting with Nona under the big maple tree nursing a baby. Kaye remembered how she felt then, when Diedra was tiny, so tired she thought she'd flop down in Nona's old green metal lawn chair and never get up again. Something like she felt now. It was way down in the fall, and there weren't many good outside sitting days left. Soon Kaye's dad would be putting the chairs under the house. Soon Pedaling Pete would be coming around asking people if he could get their leaves up. Sit while you can.

This is how Diedra saw her mother and Nona, how she expected them to be when she came home from her adventures. She would have small special somethings in the secret hidden flap of her backpack for them. Things made out of ivory or jade or gold, she would know them when she saw them.

When Big Ed showed up at the Maclellands' garage to place his order — he wanted to be special order number one — he took Diedra with him. Screw Kaye. All she had to do these days was worry; he couldn't understand what was wrong with her. And he was sorry. He'd tell you leaving Kaye was the only mistake he ever made. But it was a whopper, and it just kept on rolling, picking up bits and pieces of the rest of his life as he went along dragging that mistake behind him. Comets going through space worked this way, he thought. Maybe comets themselves were somebody's big galactic mistakes. He couldn't say for sure, would bet some psychiatrist could draw a big arcing curve from their divorce to his dropping his trou out at the golf course. Probably so. People just did shit, crazy shit, and you never really knew why. Loose wires like in the dash of his Town Car so that the idiot lights came on whenever they damn-well pleased.

He pulled up Bobby's garage door and hollered, "Let's get a look at this operation," and then he walked around bending his head over Bobby's special-made alignment jig and pulled his glasses up his nose to examine the boxes of tubes and lugs at close range. Diedra slipped around him, picking up and putting down tools, acting like she belonged there. "Nice setup," Ed said.

"Oh Daddy. Don't listen to him, Bobby, he doesn't know doodly squat."

"Hey now. You think Bobby Mac talked to his daddy like that?" Ed said even as he was remembering that Bobby didn't have a daddy long enough to smart off to. "Or his mother?" he added. But Diedra went off to the back of the garage and sat against the wall. Having her dad in Bobby Mac's shop was all wrong. Everything in there should have gotten up off the work bench and flown right out the window into the yard where it would spin into a funnel-shaped cloud and blow away. Big Ed ruined everything, Diedra thought while she half worked on a lug and listened in to Bobby Mac being all different with her father.

"You tell me," Ed said. "She's been in a pissy mood for thirteen years." Diedra knew they were talking about Kaye. Bobby Mac asked her about her mother from time to time in a tone of voice that suggested Kaye was maybe recovering from a long harrowing illness. "I'm sure she is a loving person," Bobby had told her. And Diedra said she guessed she was, though tired and in a hurry was the way she pictured her mom. Bobby Mac said nobody should be in a hurry, that everything happened whenever it happened and there was nothing you could do to change it.

"Nothing?"

"Nothing." And what she heard in his voice made her wonder if this was such a good thing or not.

Big Ed was telling Bobby, "Well, she's been worse since you came back to town. It's not your fault or anything, but it's like she wants to run the clock back."

Bobby Mac was measuring Ed with his mom's old tape measure in every possible direction, from his waist to the nape of his neck, from his elbow to his fingertips, across his shoulders and from his crotch to the floor. "Everybody wants that. It's just something you have to fight."

"Not me. Hell no. Buy a goddamn big car and drive. Am I right?"

"Or a bike."

"Oh yeah, a bike." Bobby was done with his measuring, and Ed shook himself off the way he did after he got a haircut, shaking his body all over to claim it back. "Bobby, do you eat animals anymore?"

Bobby said he had not eaten meat since he left the Air Force.

"Well shit. Too bad. You could come to the Jaycees barbecue this weekend. New businessman in town and all that." Bobby shrugged. He started walking around the garage picking stuff up and setting it down in different places.

Diedra said she wanted to go home. "You heard this one?" Ed asked him on the way out when he thought Diedra was where she couldn't hear them. "Why'd the Polack wear a black rubber?"

Bobby laughed a phony, nervous laugh and said Big Ed told him that one when they were in college.

"So what's the answer?"

"I can't remember, Ed."

"That's OK. If you can't get it in a couple of days, give me a call. I got a place down on the lake I want to get you to take a look at. Everything you need for some peace and quiet, you know?"

Bobby Mac didn't know at all. He had looked all over the world for peace and quiet and never found any of it except for an accidental minute or two here and there. Could it be it was waiting for him in a lake-front cottage outside Mooresville, North Carolina?

Hillbilly graveyard. Tombstones lean at odd angles, and the weather has worn away the lettering on the limestone slabs. You can hardly read the names and dates. Love. Eternity. Forever. *What do these things mean?* Dear Child—*all that's left to read, the name, the dates are missing. The head nicked off the little lamb footstone.* Remember me.

Nona heard it first on the CB scanner she kept going all the time. She didn't like to be morbid, but when your husband's a lineman, it only takes one mistake. Just as she was getting herself settled in front of the "Today Show," a cup of coffee and a big plastic bag full of her yarn and crochet hooks, she caught it. Something about a man dead beside the highway, something about a bicycle.

She fiddled with the scanner and tried to get it clear, to get the whole story. When she couldn't, she went ahead and called Kaye. The phone rang and rang, but Kaye was already driving Diedra to school. Then she didn't know what to do, so she called Big Ed. Then Nona did the hard but necessary thing; she went out and got in her old blue Falcon and drove the two blocks down and three blocks over to Fieldstone Drive. Somebody would have to be there when Mrs. Maclelland got the news.

An old hillbilly man out picking up aluminum cans found him. In his silvery blue tights and jersey, his white helmet like a big old broken egg, his swept-back glasses mashed against his face, Bobby Mac looked like he had fallen to earth from a passing spaceship. His bike of bent tubes and broken spokes might have been some device used for his torture and execution. Of course it wasn't so. But the old man would not touch him or even go near. Instead he stood by the road waving his arm to passing cars for an hour before somebody stopped. It didn't matter, Bobby Mac had already been dead a long time.

Now that old man sat in the back of Alvin Beale's cruiser with his trash bag of cans between his knees, sorry he said anything, sure in the end he would get the blame, when Big Ed drove up and climbed out of his Lincoln. "Hey, hey, Alvin." Ed wished he had some smokes or sticks of gum to offer around. Alvin Beale, the county deputy, had been a second-string guard on a pretty good team. He knew Ed; he probably remembered Bobby Mac. Ed was wearing a tan Ultrasuede jogging suit like he always did when he sat around in the morning with his coffee and waited for the phone to ring, "Like my pajamas?" Probably Alvin was relieved to see Ed. He had nothing to do but lean on the fender of his car with all its lights going while three carloads of state men crawled all over the accident scene. Some were patrolmen, but some were in coats and ties, and they were down the bank from where a four-by-four highway signpost was snapped clean away. Was Bobby still down there in the weeds? Had the ambulance already come and gone?

"What are they saying, Alvin?" Ed asked him.

"You could go down there; they won't mind."

But Ed already had a pretty good idea of how things worked out. Except for why. That was the thing about Bobby Mac he'd never know. You could say he'd pissed his life away: a grown man on a bicycle. Ed could see that's probably what Alvin was thinking as they stood shooting the shit, wondering out loud why there wasn't a single kid in Mooresville anymore who knew how to block down on a linebacker.

Sometimes you just wanted to stand well off, let things be, go home and pick up the morning paper where you left off. If anybody asked, you didn't see a thing. "You and me, Alvin," Ed told him and threw his hand out toward the state men, making a mark in the air, cutting them loose like an iceberg that might drift on off, carrying Alvin and him away until the cops and whatever part of Bobby that hung around this place were out of sight.

We'll never understand. Bobby Mac dead on the road and not even a skid mark, only the clipped-off signpost and his ruined bike and mashed-up organs. In his coffin he looked unmarked. He even looked relaxed in a way he never could let himself be in his walking around days. Kaye could not accept it. She wept bitterly all day and made Diedra go to school so she could give her grief full run of the house. She wasn't through with Bobby Mac, she saw that now. As long as he had been gone from Mooresville, when he had enlisted and vanished without a peep, she had not missed him at all. Somehow he was still around, still tethered, if only by his mom, to this place. He would be back; they would settle whatever there was to settle still rubbing between them. Now, suddenly there was this big hole, an emptiness she could not name and could not fill up. Just like when Diedra was born. But Diedra had started to grow into a little girl and gradually she filled up the hole. This time would be different.

Nona hated funerals, and this one was worse than most. Plenty of people came, which made up for Mrs. Raymond Maclelland's not having much family but her son, the lawyer, and his wife, who used to be so pretty but now was looking as stiff and hard as Mrs. Mac. They didn't have any kids. Mrs. Maclelland's former students came, and some people who knew Bobby, though nobody in town really knew him anymore. Big Ed found some pallbearers, God knows where, some old boys he shot golf with maybe. Even the preacher, a Presbyterian boy fresh faced from seminary and not knowing a thing about the varieties of terrible death and knowing less about the soul he was eulogizing, was a letdown. He wandered around in his platitudes for twenty-five minutes inventing a Bobby Mac full of human kindness, courage, grace and eternal hope. All hooey, Nona thought. Now was the time to show some respect for the dead and not go on making up lies about them. Bobby Mac was a sweet boy who might have gotten his life together if he'd had another ten years or so to work on it. She sat there getting mad and fidgety and started feeling sorry she hadn't thought to bring something to crochet on. As she went on and on in her head about respect for the dead, she remembered what was the end to Big Ed's dirty joke. Well, she had never thought that joke was funny anyway.

After the service Kaye snuck into Mrs. Mac's garage while the others were in the house eating and tried to find Bobby's notebook. But she was too slow. Everything was gone: the books, the hammock, the grass mat. Gone to the Goodwill Store. Even the tools and tubes for bicycle frames were all stacked on the heavy table. Before the week was out, a guy from Charlotte would pick them up. He'd bought the whole lot over the phone. Mrs. Mac saved that notebook, didn't she? Kaye knew. There was no point asking about it; she'd deny ever having seen it. She wouldn't even read it, but put it away in a drawer and never take it out.

Right across the road from the accident site, there was a patch of kudzu vines, acres deep, acres long. It had covered up all the trees, barns, telephone lines, and fences. It had hidden all the junked cars and abandoned appliances people had dumped there. Diedra made Big Ed drive her to the spot after the funeral. When she saw it, she thought it would have reminded Bobby of the temple called Angkor Wat. He told her about seeing it, about how it had all been allowed to go back to jungle until some Frenchman uncovered it again. Its walls were the mountains at the end of the world. Beyond them, every step had meaning in it; every step was the history of all time with people doing bad or doing good.

Imagine, he told her, what it must have been like when they started pulling the vines away. A holy city might be buried anywhere, then, mightn't it?

There was still plenty of food. Big Ed filled up his Blue Willow plate with slices of turkey and ham, a few deviled eggs, some asparagus casserole, baked beans, and glazed apples. He would have to come back and get some cake later. He went back in the living room and looked around. Nobody was left but Nona and Kaye and Mrs. Mac. What a sad crew. Three broken-hearted people sitting around trying to think of something to say. "Hey, listen," he said to them. "What'd the Buddhist monk order from the hot dog stand?"

That Ed. You got to love him.

Trip to Sometimes Island

Not everybody brought a float. Rick Nix didn't bring one. But he had sat on the lakeshore blowing up the three Barb brought along, passing through a stage that reminded him pleasantly of long make-out sessions with his high school girlfriend and going on to the point where his face was purple and his mouth was numb. He felt like that gave him the right to pick up the red one, the flimsiest—a one-person float at best—and walk into the lake with it. Now he was lying about thirty yards offshore staying alert. You never could tell when somebody might catch a cramp or a little kid wander out over his head, and Rick wanted to be the one to the rescue. Pulling the gasping party onto the beach, he would set him down among his silly half-wasted friends with a gesture almost of contempt for their carelessness. Then he'd go back to Annie and Barb and the guy—what was his name, Gibson? All day people would be pointing him out, talking about him, but Rick Nix would keep it focused, focused on being Rick Nix. He considered for a moment that this was how it must be for professional athletes, guys who couldn't even go by a drive-through window without somebody wanting a piece of them. For now, nothing was actually happening, but at any minute one of the windsurfers could clobber somebody with his board, a motorboat might drift inside the buoys. You just never knew.

Maybe twenty yards to Rick's right, Barb and Annie lay crosswise on the fancy silver float with the clear tuck and roll top, kicking from time to time, talking in a lazy way. Rick couldn't hear what they said, but he bet they were talking about him. Annie was telling Barb all about him.

Barb came out to the lake every chance she could, so she kept the floats in her trunk. Lately, Gibson had been coming along with her. He was house-sitting the place down the way where he was trying to finish his doctoral dissertation on cowboys and the economics of the Old West. At first Barb thought he was making this up. Cowboys, really. Then she felt sorry for him because he had been working on this thing for years, reading and reading and making boxes of note cards that seemed about to push him right out the door of his small, hot place. But it seemed like there was always more to read, more to consider. Gibson was trying to quit smoking and that was how they got together. Barb had been trying for years. Gibson said they could start a buddy system. Whenever one of them was dying for a cigarette, they could just pick up the phone for help. And Gibson was clever and sometimes witty.

He was on his back on a bright blue raft rolling in the chop made by the motorboats, probably thinking about the dusty trail to Abilene. How many cows, how many riders? How many of those cows wound up in a boxcar on the railroad and how many of them were vulture food? He was smiling, his tufts of red hair and his little round sunglasses and pointy nose bobbing in and out of sight. He was cute for a thirty-five-year-old man.

Rick Nix was another story. Barb had to wonder where Annie found them. This was what she wanted to tell her, but first she thought she ought to at least listen to how they met and why this one was the one when he looked so much like the rest.

"He fixes these sports cars up and sells them," Annie said. "He just parks them out in his yard with a For Sale sign on them and they practically sell themselves to these frat boys and real estate agents who want something to play around in."

"I get that, Annie, but what does he do?"

Annie told Barb again that fixing cars was what Rick Nix *did* do. There was money in it, all kinds once you worked your way up to the real high-dollar cars—old Jaguars and Mercedes two-seaters.

Right then a little bit of hell broke loose on the beach. Actually it wasn't what you would call a beach but a series of big limestone rocks that came down to the water like king-sized stairs. All kinds of people were sitting and lying on the rocks because it was Sunday afternoon in Texas and the temperature was somewhere over a hundred degrees.

These kids, maybe nineteen or twenty, a boy and a girl, were getting all over each other. Hollering right up in each other's faces. He said she didn't know what she wanted, and she said she did too, that she wanted to be left alone. He wondered what she had invited him out here for anyway if not to humiliate him in front of her friends. She said he had been acting terrible all day. Gradually the boy got madder. He was a regular Texas boy wearing cutoff jeans and an indistinguishable tattoo on his right bicep, no earrings or strange-looking hair. Rick Nix could see he might be a good-looking boy if you straightened his face out from the twisty way he was holding it now.

After he called her a bitch and told her to fuck herself, the boy didn't know anything else to say. If he could let go like a fire whistle and scream, that might do the trick, but twenty years of tight-lipped Texas male-hood wouldn't let him do anything like that.

"Thanks for ruining my birthday," she told him. She was already crying. Annie and Barb could tell tears were slipping down her face even if they couldn't see them. But now she started bawling in earnest, in broad daylight for a couple of hundred strangers to see.

"Oh go to hell, I'm leaving," the boy told her because it seemed like there was nothing else he could do. And he walked up the dry scrabble ground, under the trees and out of sight.

The place was quiet, the way any place is after a disaster strikes. The girl sat in her fold-out chaise lounge and kept on crying. She wore the smallest of bikinis, coffee-colored to match her tan. With everybody looking-but-not-looking at her now, she got up and pulled a T-shirt with the arms ripped out over herself. She might as well be naked, and it was his T-shirt too, everybody could see that.

"Gosh, buckaroos and buckarettes, wasn't that distressing?" Gibson had suddenly come to life and was sitting astride his raft bronco-busting style, riding the waves closer to the two women.

"Gibson," Barb said, "you wouldn't do something like that, would you?"

"Well, no." And he meant it; he wouldn't do anything like that *now*. But what had brought him up out of his daydream—not a daydream of cowboys heeding the invisible hand of supply and demand as they watched for rustlers cutting into their profit margin, but a daydream of an unfiltered Pall Mall cigarette—was the recognition of the scene playing out on the shore in front of him. It was in the cadence of the sentences as much as the words, which were much harsher than any he would have used. He heard himself in the boy and felt his face redden just as it had back when? And what had it been about, that fight that came rolling upon him and the slight, pretty girl in her white blouse with the Peter Pan collar, rolling out of nowhere like a tornado? He could not remember; he could only see the aftermath in his high school cafeteria where he retreated sullenly among the stag boys who ate at the long tables by the windows while she ran out to the bathroom escorted by her closest friends. Their trays of half-eaten chili beans with wadded up napkins all around would stay on the table after the bell rang, and the girl's desk would be empty in geometry class.

If Annie heard the "no" in Gibson's answer, Barb hung on the "well." Something was in there when a man said "well" since he found it easy enough to say an ordinary "no" whenever he really wanted to. She looked hard across Annie's back at Gibson, whose look of dopey denial said she was right.

"The thing is," Gibson said, "you can't get around hurting people sometimes. You just can't; it's the way you learn."

"Is it, Gibson? Is that how it goes?" Barb said. "Like something off the Discovery Channel?" She lowered her voice and said in a confidential monotone, "'Here's the baby coyote gnawing the leg off the half-dead rabbit while the wise old coyote looks on approvingly.' We learn by doing?"

"That's not fair. You know what I mean. Falling in love is a trial-and-error thing."

"Lots of errors," Barb said.

Rick Nix, not liking the sound of this talk, used his hands to fin himself out to deeper water. Flat on his belly on his raft, he was looking and listening, looking at the legs of the two women as they occasionally paddled their raft, following the movement of their muscles from their calves to their thighs and on to where the fabric of their suits stretched across their bottoms. And he was listening for the sound of the boy's car at full throttle in low range ripping up the narrow road from the lake. It was in just this way that a good boy who had nothing in mind when this day began but going to the lake and having a few beers with his sweetie could end up ruining himself.

Somehow he was to blame, right? Rick Nix had been getting these negative vibes from Barb ever since they met up at her house, a little house down off the side of Mount Bonnell in a pocket of old frame houses that somehow got away from the developers. All Barb had added was a Jacuzzi built right into the private deck. "Hey, you could get nekkid and jump in that anytime you wanted, huh?" he said.

"It's not working," she said, and somehow made it clear in three words that the thought of sitting in a Jacuzzi naked with Rick Nix might make her sick. OK, if that's how she wanted to be. But she had a nice place, a place just for one, and Rick could tell from the framed pictures on the walls and the matching chair and couch—not the same old junk he saw in everybody else's place in town—that Barbara was a classy lady, and for Annie's sake, he was going to try not to let her piss him off.

He knew this trip to the lake was a kind of test. Barb was Annie's best friend from way back; now she was some kind of junior hotshot with the government, made good money and didn't have to answer her own phone. Naturally, she would look down her nose at Rick Nix. But with a busted radiator hose in the middle of nowhere, who would you rather be with—Rick or that Gibson guy?

For Annie, that was an easy one. There was something pleasing about going over to Rick's place in the middle of town where he rented both the garage and the apartment above it. He had everything he needed right there in the garage where the places for his tools were drawn in Magic Marker on a pegboard and always put back at the end of a job, where Rick did everything to get a car in shape except paint it. He hired that out, he told her, though he did the body work and priming himself. "These days you know what they say, 'You're only as good as your car,'" Rick Nix told her, and Annie was charmed by the conviction in his voice.

Annie wasn't a dummy. She was tired of guys like Gibson, guys who spent two hours every Saturday morning crawling over the newspaper when you could be out going to yard sales and having fun, guys who scratched their flaky scalps and picked their noses when it was only just the two of you. Listen, she wanted to say to Barb, there are types and there are types.

About then the boy came back out from under the trees. He hadn't gone anywhere at all and from the look of his face maybe he had been crying too. But now he was in control of himself—a little shaky, but in control. When he got about twenty feet from the girl, who sat in her lounge sniffling and watching the lake from behind dark glasses, he hollered, "Hey." She jerked around; he said, "Another thing, don't expect me to be coming back around."

While several people including Gibson and Barb sniggered, the girl just stared until one of her friends propped herself up on her beach towel and said, "Go on, Darrell, can't you see?" He did go on, back under the trees, though whether he saw what the girls expected him to see was anybody's guess.

All the way up the winding road that went from the lake to the highway along the ridge top, Rick Nix looked for the boy's telltale skid marks. It was like somebody had stuck his head in a bell and rung it. That boy could have been him. He thought of the first car he'd ever fixed up, a white 1963 Impala. Cruising that car with his girl sitting curled in the seat beside him, he looked out on his little Texas town like a king. Then they'd disappear out into the country to the little places he knew and pull off. That's where they fought at first, and she made him take her back to the drive-in where he felt like a character in a play. Other kids sat on the hoods of cars or looked out the windows while just the two of them yelled at each other, their shadows made twenty feet long by the streetlights around the place, until her friends swooped in and folded her into the back seat of some girl's daddy's Buick. Since then, Rick Nix thought, how much in his life had changed?

For one thing he had gotten married. And two years later he got divorced, which was something he hadn't told Annie. Divorce really scared them off; it said you'd screwed up big time. Rick didn't think so at all; it was more like planting a plant that didn't quite take hold. He thought of the girl—because that's what his wife was and he was still a boy—as somebody he had roomed with a couple of years. They got up and ate together and went out the door and came home and ate together, then laid on their busted-down couch watching TV until it was time for bed. There had been some stuff, wedding present stuff like a blender and a microwave, stuff that seemed to have disappeared out of his life just like she had.

He tried to remember their fights, but he could only remember what they had them over—who washed the dishes and who cleaned up the house. He could not see himself or the girl the way he could his high school girlfriend and now himself in the parking lot of the drive-in. As if he hovered somewhere above that scene, he saw his car skidded to a stop, both doors open and the red interior bleeding out into the damp summer air. She threw her arms out at him and her mouth snapped like a cornered animal's. "'Shit, shit, shit," Rick Nix mumbled and looked out Barb's back seat window.

If he'd had his way, he would have said to drive on back to town; it was Barb who wanted to stop at the Oasis for beer and some nachos. Rick would have said he was sick of Barb and Gibson, but really he was sick for that boy and a little for that girl, sick for the way he used to be and could never be again. He pointed his chair out toward the lake, pulled the brim of his ball cap low, and looked out through his dark glasses.

"You know you can see the sunset twice out here," Gibson said. "You stare at the sun right as it drops into the water, and you'll see another green sun just above it." Annie and Barb started staring earnestly at the sun. "You might have to take your sunglasses off," Gibson said. Rick Nix sat there with his glasses on.

"Hey, yeah," Barb said, "there it was. I saw it. Did you see it, Annie?"

Annie said she hadn't but would keep looking.

"You can't. It's too late now," Gibson said. "It's like those illusions that used to be in comic books when we were kids. You look at the green pig on the black background for thirty seconds, then you look up at the ceiling and see a red pig. You hold the image on your retina for a while." Barb beamed at Annie. See, she was thinking, see? See what a neat guy Gibson is?

And Gibson, feeling the warm radiance of the two women's approval, went on talking. "See right out there in front of the dam? There's an island there—you can't see it now because the water is high, but when the level drops, it comes out. Sometimes Island."

"Bull," said Rick Nix. "There's no island out there. Look at the slope of the land dropping down into the water. It's got to be a couple of hundred feet deep out there."

"It's there," said Gibson, "check a map sometime."

Whenever something ugly like this happened, Annie blamed herself. Maybe it had been a mistake to bring Rick and Gibson along when they had never met each other. But it mattered. If Rick was the one, and she has been thinking for a while he might be, then he had to get along with Barb. But now she wondered what she really knew about him. They had eaten out in nice places and gone to the movies—Rick's kind of movies, cops and robbers things, spy stuff. She even rode up to Dallas with him to a sports car meet where he bought some bumpers and a carburetor for an MG he was working on.

Mostly that trip had gone OK. They had fun on the drive bouncing up the interstate in Rick's truck with the windows down and country music going full blast on the tape deck. And when they got there, Rick turned out to be a smart, slick dealer. Which was a relief. For a while, Annie had worried that Rick had a part in his brain that made him a clever mechanic inside an otherwise simple guy. Now she saw his brain as a complex system of parts availabilities, labor time, and market values. He didn't make money by accident.

But he pulled into the Broken Arrow Motor Court, a place with half a dozen black and chrome motorcycles parked on its asphalt apron, thinking to spend the night. A place where drug deals no doubt went down at all hours, where doors slammed, people yelled, and the air conditioner broke. That was their first near-fight. When they had finally settled into bed at the Econolodge, Rick eased back to his own gentle self. It was only thirty dollars difference they were talking about.

Annie grabbed Rick by the arm and squeezed it; he sat there like he had turned into a piece of limestone rock. If it had only been the two of them, she would have reached up and taken off those glasses and pushed that hat back. Such a move seemed to be too dangerous now, so she said, "Why don't you tell them what kind of car you're working on now?"

"MGB," Rick mumbled.

"Oh, I always wanted one of those," Barb said. Annie could see she was trying to help.

"No you don't."

"OK, why don't I?"

"It's a piece of junk."

"But it won't be after you fix it up, will it?"

"It was junk the day they made it. No matter how much work I do on it, it'll stay the same."

"Wow," said Gibson. "That is remarkable. Do people know they're getting a lousy car? I bet they do. And they buy it anyway. There are inverse variables in economics, you know, having to do with quality and price and demand. But to pay a high price for poor quality—what would that mean?" His voice faded out, and Annie had to wonder if Gibson hadn't gone sliding down one of his economic curves out of sight.

"The world is fucked," Rick Nix told him. "That's not news."

Not news to Rick Nix or even to Barb, who was a bureaucrat after all, or to Gibson, who in his heart of hearts knew all economics was voodoo, but maybe to Annie it was. She ought to have known better. But for years she had looked into a world where people stopped on red and went on green, where they returned her lost checkbooks, pocketbooks, and keys. She had loved more men than she cared to remember, yet each time it went haywire another one came along and she made him her famous apple pancakes and swore her love anew. Just because it hadn't been the real thing yet didn't mean the real thing wasn't going to happen.

"Oh," she said, "let's go home." The nachos were cold and the pitcher of beer was gone. Nobody should have drunk beer after sitting out in the sun all afternoon anyhow. That's what set them off, that and those poor kids fighting. Better that they should all go home and start over in the morning.

———————

Barb and Annie stretched themselves out on the hood of Barb's car, their backs against the windshield, their heads resting against their rolled-up beach towels, both looking at the sky. Even this far out of town, the stars at night weren't as big and bright as you'd expect them to be. Maybe if they tried, they could pick out the Big Dipper. That was the extent of Barb and Annie's knowledge of stars, but it really didn't matter; they'd come to see a meteor shower. Gibson told Barb about it and invited her to ride out and look with him, but she told him she had to work. Now she felt a little guilty.

"He's a sweet guy," Annie said. "Are you sleeping with him?"

"God. Yeah. Once. Remember last time we came out to the lake? That night. I felt sorry for him, and we had a couple of more beers when we got back."

"Sorry."

"Oh, cut it out. It's not your fault. It's not even that Nixon's . . ."

"Nix."

"Whatever. It's not his fault. We're all grown-ups. I just wish Gibson would finish that damned dissertation and get on with his life. Or just quit. Give it up. It's got him so paralyzed."

"What will he do when he finishes?"

"Madame Annie sees into the future, and there he is—Gibson, one baby step farther along in his life, but still the same Gibson."

Annie didn't say anything. But Gibson had reminded her too much of the sports reporter with the drinking problem, the splenetic English instructor, guys who had names but were more easily remembered by their symptoms. "So see, Rick isn't that way."

"Right-o, he's not that way. He's a slam-it-in-gear and patch-out sort of guy. Haven't you had enough of them too? I mean, he's just like that boy we saw at the lake. Still messing with cars, still catching the ball games, still living his Joe Bachelor life."

"That poor, poor girl," Annie said; she could still see her goose bumps as she sat there shivering on a hundred degree day.

"Boohoohoo. I bet you could go out to Windy Point the very next day, or the day after, and if not Windy Point some other place on the lake and see those two sitting there with their cooler of beer like nothing ever happened." It was like boxing had been in the early days, Barb thought, when people were knocked down and got back up and went on hitting each other again and again until only one was left standing. Only this was true love. "Lots of internal bleeding. You can't see it but it's there."

"Oh shoot, there goes one." A meteor cut across the sky, making a bright orange trail. If Gibson had been along, he would have told them that meant there was a lot of iron in it. But Annie was thinking that you should be holding a button. Hold a button when you see a shooting star, make a wish and you'll get it. Barb said no, that was for when you drove under a railroad bridge with a train going over it. All you had to do to be lucky with shooting stars was to see one. Besides, Annie was lucky already.

"How? How am I lucky?"

"Your psyche is still in one piece. You aren't a single mom living in a trailer court." By those standards, Barb was lucky too. She knew this, but wasn't it right to expect something more, something from love? What she had in mind was Sartre and de Beauvoir lying in bed after great sex, smoking those terrific French cigarettes and talking. Talking about great literature and great art, about politics and action as the salvation from despair. From what she had read, though, Jean-Paul was no better than the rest of them.

Neither was Gibson. He was the one who reminded her of how great a cigarette was after sex. There were only two times she craved one, then and when she was working on her computer where she kept packs of Lifesavers and bubble gum to protect her. In bed, she suddenly found herself vulnerable, and Gibson, who was supposed to be her helping hand, was the one who suggested she dig out the stash she kept somewhere in her house in case of an emergency. He knew she had one. When she produced half a pack of stale Marlboro Lights from a discarded purse, he lit one for both of them, took a drag, said, "God, these are awful," and sucked the smoke to the bottom of his lungs.

She didn't hate Gibson, but resented the hell out of him for exposing her in her weakness. It was like a late movie dialogue where the broken, weeping female lead tells the sodden, rumpled male lead she's no good for him, and he completes the litany by assuring her that he's no good either. But together . . . together they'll be no damn good together. "I don't want to see Gibson anymore, but now he feels like he can drop in anytime my car is in the driveway," Barb told Annie.

"He's OK. You just have to push the right buttons with a guy like him. Give him a little confidence."

"You're no help." More than anything, Barb wanted to reach into her purse and get a cigarette out of the new fresh pack. But she didn't want Annie to know she was smoking again.

Another shooting star went over. "You know what we ought to do? We ought to hold hands or stick our fingers in each other's navels or something so when the next one goes over half of my brain will go in your head and half of your brain will go in mine. That way I'll have better sense, and you'll have some hope."

"Hope. Good Lord, Annie."

A couple of miles away Gibson sat in the open door of his Ford Escort with the dome light turned off, looking for meteors. Between his legs was a quart of cheap beer in a paper sack. If Barb had come along, he would have bought something nicer. People forgot he was a graduate student; hell, he was trying to forget himself but couldn't quite bring it off.

Gibson had probably driven right past Annie and Barb but didn't see them because he was brooding too hard on how he had pissed Barbara off. She hadn't said anything, but he knew. Maybe it had been a case of bad timing, which made it all the worse. Gibson thought he had a gift for listening, for saying the right thing, for averting a crisis with a clever line. It was an art form, a skill, even if it wasn't especially marketable.

"*Je t'aime*," he'd told Barb as they lay in the bed smoking and began humming, "do dum da da da da da, do dum dum da da da da da," his version of the theme from *A Man and a Woman*.

"Oh, Gibson, cut it out."

Right then, he thought. Right then he had crossed some invisible line and whatever they had or were about to have began to come apart. What could have been more appropriate than a French movie about sex and smoking and driving cars? Barb only complained that the cigarette made her woozy. "They're bad for you, I hear," he told her, but she didn't think that was funny either.

He looked into the starry sky and thought of Rick Nix and his sports cars, and he thought of his miserable dissertation. It occurred to him that once upon a time people ate beans mostly or rice and didn't see a thing wrong with it, that eating a hunk of beef every day was something they had talked themselves into. Beef was something just a few people got to eat and as a result everybody else got so they wanted it. And they talked themselves into liking what? He pictured a rare steak on a plate oozing greasy blood; he imagined a gristly piece in his mouth expanding with every bite until it felt like a big wad of cardboard. Somehow he got it down, his neck expanding in the effort—ooong—like a cartoon character's. Love was like that. Love was something people didn't need but talked themselves into. It probably wasn't any better for you than steak, Gibson thought. But he didn't believe it.

He thought of Barb's friend Annie, who wasn't as sexy as Barb was in her heels and stockings and tailored skirts, but seemed to radiate a comforting warmth. There she was tangled up with that ass Rick Nix, a true primitive capitalist if there ever was one. He ought to have Caveat Emptor tattooed on his backside. But in his half-educated redneck way, Rick was the better economist. He knew the rock bottom of buying and selling didn't have a thing to do with need. Lust, venality, greed—that's what drove the market, that's what the world was all about.

Even the meteor shower was a bust. Gibson saw seven or eight in an hour. He decided it was just as well Barb hadn't come along. She would have expected the sky to be filled with balls of fire. She would have expected more than he could deliver.

In his garage, Rick Nix was torquing down the cylinder head on the MGB he was fixing. Contrary to what anybody thought, he would have been interested in seeing a meteor shower if he'd known there was one going on right overhead. One thing about growing up poor in a state where everybody who could drove Cadillacs or Lincolns was that it taught you to appreciate what you could get for free, whether it was a shiny hubcap in the ditch or a shooting star up in the sky. You could get a bunch of hubcaps together and hang them in a tree or on the fence and have your own set of constellations. Not that Rick Nix knew about constellations any more than Annie or Barb did. But he thought about them differently. He wasn't ashamed of what he didn't know. If he didn't know it and was getting along OK without it, which he was, then he didn't need it. That's what he told Annie. "GED? What do I want with a GED?"

Annie knew she couldn't tell Barb that Rick Nix never finished high school. Barb would tell Gibson. It would prove he had no ambition, which wasn't true at all.

Rick Nix got his hands on a Jag XK-140 once. Now that car was something. To go scooting around the Hill Country back roads in that thing, to watch every old boy's jaw drop when he passed them, hell, even the cows took notice. But that Jaguar was a burden. To keep it pretty, to keep it running sharp, just to sit in it at a traffic light took something out of him. Rick Nix had to let that car go. When he did, he turned some good money, almost enough to let him forget about what it had been like to take it out in the middle of the night, turn on the headlights and fog lights, and run the hell out of it.

Rick Nix didn't mind Annie hanging around while he was working. That's when he told her about the Jag. He would like to have seen her right then sitting on one of the old railroad ties that ran along the edge of the driveway, her skirt not quite gathered up under her, laughing at his stories. When he thought about that Jag, he had to laugh too. He took Annie's laughter to mean that she understood the stories the same way he did, but in this he was mistaken.

Here is the kind of story Rick Nix liked to tell Annie while he worked: This boy he grew up with had gotten ahold of a wrecked, but practically brand-new, Pontiac Lemans, a car he bought—totaled—from an insurance man for fifty dollars. Salvage value. He had taken that car; it had been rolled; it was a mess; that car didn't have a straight piece of metal on it. And, little by little, that boy put that car back so solid you would have to have a real good eye to even see it had ever been wrecked at all. It had a bent frame though, and you never could tell what would happen when you straightened a bent frame. Going straight one minute, down the highway sideways the next. Anyway, he drove it around about a week and sold it. While he was thinking about what to do next, whether to find another insurance car, or something easier, or go to work for his uncle driving a semi-truck, he was thumbing along the highway and got run down by a car.

"Was it the same car? He got run over by his own car?"

"No. It was just a car."

Annie didn't get it. Rick Nix might tell this kind of story while rolled under a car on his creeper, reaching for the next sentence in the same way his hand came out from under the car and groped for the wrench he needed. What was that supposed to mean? Rick Nix didn't know either, it seemed. It was just another of his stories where one of his friends ended up getting killed or maimed or finding six hundred dollars in a Prince Albert can in a box of junk. When she added all his stories up, it seemed like he lived in a world where almost everybody he knew was killed in a freak accident or struck by some weird disease or newly rich and living in a new double-wide trailer on a hill.

"You could open a foreign car repair place," she told him.

"Why would I want to do that?" The idea seemed to offend Rick Nix.

Barb saw the little blue car parked facing the road in Annie's complex with the For Sale sign in the window. One phone number was Annie's so the other one had to be Rick Nix's. Probably she shouldn't have said anything; she had told herself she wouldn't, but when Annie let her in, she had the phone tucked against her cheek and was saying, "Well it's a 1978, and it has about eighty thousand miles and a new clutch and a new top, lots of other new parts too, good tires."

Annie paused while the person on the other end asked something, and said, "Right, he's in the Air Force and being sent overseas so he has to let it go. He loves that car. It'll break his heart."

"You're lying for him," Barb said when she hung up.

"Oh," Annie said, "I know it's bad, but Rick can't guarantee these cars—you know how boys will drive a car—and this way if something goes wrong, there won't be as many questions."

Rick Nix liked this arrangement. Annie's place was a better location for people to see his cars, and Annie was a better person to do the talking too. She didn't know squat about a car so when a potential buyer quizzed her she didn't even have to be evasive. "I love the color," she would say. "It's awfully fun riding around with the top down." But the brakes? The suspension? She just didn't know.

Barb thought about calling Rick Nix and telling him a thing or two, but he wouldn't have understood. He was just doing what old boys in his family had always done, first with horses, then with cars. Talking out under a big shade tree, buying, selling, trading. Sometimes you came out all right, sometimes you lost your ass, but as long as everybody played the game . . .

This is how he met Annie, who was in charge of the classified section of the *American Statesman*. One of her people put his Triumph Spitfire ad under motorcycles instead of cars, something they did about once a week it seemed. Rick Nix called and then came around and pitched a fit about the ad until he got his money back. Then he asked Annie out and she agreed. She went because she thought it took some self-respect, maybe even courage, for a country-acting guy in a gimmie cap to come down to the paper's fancy building by the lake and stick up for himself. Rick Nix did not tell her that he sold the car anyhow, that in his mind this had been a lucky day: sold the car, got his twenty-five dollars back, and got a date with a pretty woman. The money he spent on dinner that night wasn't even out of pocket, strictly speaking.

Which didn't mean that what he felt for Annie wasn't an honest kind of affection or that he wasn't pleased with the way one of his overhauled cars looked shined and waxed and parked at a jaunty angle with its For Sale sign in the window. What it did mean was harder to explain; in fact, Rick Nix had never really stopped to consider it.

"He doesn't have a world view," Barb told Annie. "I bet he doesn't even know who the governor is."

"He does too." The governor was a woman, and Rick Nix made a point of saying something mocking about her every day. Annie knew this meant he cared about her, Annie; what he really thought of the governor was harder to say. "And besides, what difference does it make? You talk to Gibson about politics and I talk to Rick about cars. What are we really talking about anyway?"

Arguing with Annie was impossible. The trouble with her had always been how little she would settle for. Her nowhere job at the paper, a string of worthless guys. Rick Nix could have been the worst, for on top of having no world view he had no health insurance, retirement plan, or any plan for a future at all beyond buying and selling his next car.

Annie told Barb that Rick was planning to start a foreign car repair business. She pictured him in a natty blue jumpsuit with "Rick" stitched into the white oval over his heart. She pictured him with employees and getting respect from the rich people who bought expensive cars but didn't know how to maintain them. People respected you for what you knew; Annie believed that. "He's so smart," she told Barb. "He has an amazing memory full of all these little parts and numbers you need to know when you start adjusting engines. He just knows them."

Barb was not impressed. Gibson, for example, knew all sorts of things. Rogers Hornsby, a famous baseball player, was buried in Texas, he told her the other day just out of the blue, thinking maybe she would want to ride out and see his grave. Men handed you information, engine displacements, batting averages, because they thought if they knew enough of these things the world would make sense when stuck together by sheer fact, and women would love them for making it make sense.

Yet wasn't poor Gibson suffocated by facts? Wasn't she? Her outer office was lined with banks of file cabinets, a fortress of facts standing between her and any innocent citizen who happened to wander in looking for information on Work Force Development in the state of Texas. She had news for people; inside every fact was another pile of facts. She envied Annie, who was still able to wish upon a star, to jump over facts and believe that Rick Nix could run a small business, believe that he could make her happy the rest of her days.

Annie had grown too wary to admit such a thing to Barb, but she believed it nonetheless. Not that Rick Nix could make her happy the rest of her days, but that *she* could make them both happy. She would manage the office and would have a coverall just like Rick's with "Annie" in the oval over her heart. She had an abandoned gas station at 38th and Lamar already picked out for Rick's business. All this from watching Rick Nix peel an apple in one continuous band while she prepared the batter for her famous apple pancakes.

There was, of course, a rub. Rick Nix had his reasons for not wanting to open a shop. He didn't just work on his own cars for resale. Every now and then he did valve jobs, ring jobs, clutches, and what-have-you for cash, just between him and whoever. And out in the country behind his cousin's barn he kept about twenty old sports cars for parts. The cousin grew a little weed, and sometimes Rick Nix helped distribute some of that. He would never feel the need to fill Annie in on his complicated financial arrangements; he would josh her along until she got tired of talking about his shop.

When Barb pulled into her driveway, she found Gibson had set up his $3.99 grill on her deck. "Perfect timing," he yelled. The coals were hot and he had two New York strips ready to go. "I thought a Gamay Beaujolais would go good in this heat. And a salad."

It was hard to be mad at him; she wouldn't have to cook, didn't really have anything to cook. But then she saw his Pall Malls and lighter beside her lounge chair on the deck. "Oh no you don't, Gibson. This isn't what you think; you caught me in a moment of weakness the other night."

"That?" he said, following her look to the cigarettes. "We can quit again right now. Cold turkey." Taking up the nearly full pack, he soaked it with charcoal lighter and set it on fire in the gravel of Barb's driveway. He watched it burn with a grieved look on his face. "Who do I remind you of, Jimi Hendrix or Peter Townshend?"

"How about one of the kids in *Children of the Damned*? Gibson, we have to have a serious talk," she said.

"Right. Serious." But he did not look at her. Instead, he began dicing the vegetables for the salad on the cutting board he'd brought out from her kitchen. "I got an e-mail message today from one of my old grad-school buddies. He's in Indonesia working for Exxon, making big bucks."

"So why don't you join him? They're probably looking for somebody just like you."

"It turns out maybe I could," he said. Then Gibson considered what Barb was saying. It's true, he had long ago given up on love, if by love you meant a white hot yearning, sex in the shower, sailboats at sunset sort of thing. But he had not given up on a Nick and Nora Charles notion of love as clever repartee, owning a charming pet, and moments of witty affection. "I would probably have to finish my dissertation."

"Oh, that."

He heard what she meant. Not only was finishing the dissertation as likely as the two steaks' standing up and mooing, but she couldn't wait for her associate professor neighbor to come back home and banish Gibson to his near-campus graduate hovel, safely out of her field of vision forever. Wait a minute, he wanted to say. Maybe this was just the tail-end of a bad day. Maybe she should catch herself before she said something she would regret.

Gibson was right; Barb would come to regret this evening. Years later she would see herself in her dotted-swiss dress sitting in her lounge chair dying for a cigarette but knowing this was it, the end. That was what she would come back to again and again, the moment of sweet agony that came from wanting something utterly bad for you and telling yourself you couldn't have it.

Gibson, though, would not get to play the innocent bystander. He uncorked the wine and offered a glass to her, swirling it to bring the aroma up to her nose. "Listen, Gibson," she said, "let's eat your steaks, and then you'll go to your place and I'll stay here. We'll just cool it."

On a windless, humid night with only the sound of an occasional passing car to ease the silence, Barb was surprised to hear how much noise two people could make while eating. The snick of the steak knives cutting through the sweet rare meat, the ping of the wine glasses against the wooden deck, their jaws munching through the salad greens. She told Gibson the wine was an excellent choice, and he thanked her. His manners really were impeccable now that she had practically cut off his balls.

When Gibson finally left, she knew she would cry and wish for a cigarette more than ever. Instead, she would have to make do with walking the floor and a good stiff drink. "Gibson, don't you want to yell at me, to call me a bitch or something?"

"That's one way of doing it."

She knew what he meant. To scream and holler, break the glasses and the plates, to make recriminating calls at all hours until the other party disconnected the phone. To drive it out of your system as quickly as possible. The other way, though, was to gently, gently lull yourself with memory and regret, little ripples of hope that gradually faded away.

"You're not the type to change your mind," he told her, and she agreed he was right.

"You're not the type for regrets either." Was this true too? She could already see Gibson reduced to a cocktail party anecdote: the funny little guy with the cowboy dissertation he never could finish. But in some grander, more global way, she had her regrets. The world was full of Gibsons, which was to say it was devoid of what she imagined love to be.

Barb would marry an urbane, sophisticated man twenty years her senior who had finished his dissertation long ago and turned it into a book among his other books until he grew bored with them, who traveled widely and whose judgment was valued in and out of the great state of Texas. He also screwed every office assistant and secretary who ever crossed his path and expected Barb to put up with it because their marriage was not the bourgeois pedestrian kind.

Gibson would marry an Indonesian girl, docile and bright and from a good family. A girl who thought everybody from America was a cowboy, even Gibson.

Although the steak he grilled was very good indeed, he knew he had lost his taste for the meat even as he ate it. He quietly excused himself and went back to his temporary home where he put on a Marty Robbins recording of songs of the Wild West, sat through it until he could sing along with Marty on "The Streets of Laredo," and put himself to bed.

———————

Now it was moving into fall, the leaves were turning, and the pecans were falling all around Annie's apartment. She told Rick Nix she would make him a pecan pie if he would gather the pecans, and he came back with a bushel basket full. It turned out he loved pecan pie. He slept over whenever she could talk him into it, and sometimes Annie stayed at his place so they could get an early start on one of his weekend parts trips. But something was not right.

Rick Nix would only wear blue jeans, cowboy boots, and snap button shirts. Every morning he put on a cap from a pile of gimmie caps, each one with greasy fingerprints on the bill and a smudge of dirt right on top of the crown from looking into car engines. He didn't like any vegetables, not even lettuce, and would eat hamburgers or pizza every night of the world if it was left up to him. Annie knew what Barb would tell her, that she could do better. But she had considered these physical manifestations of Rick's hard limits along with others that were more abstract and more troubling—his taste in movies, for instance; his willingness to dismiss people like Gibson out of hand—and decided she could put up with them. Actually, she thought, everybody had limits, and seeing them right out in the open where you could name them and eventually talk about them might make things easier. Besides, Rick Nix had his points. He was neat; he treated his many neighborhood cats with benign indifference and occasionally gave them scraps of lunch meat; he was generous with his time, even if he wasn't with his money. And although he hadn't really said it in so many words, Annie knew he loved her.

What she expected was some necessary next step. She had traveled this road before, had traveled it even farther. She had been ready to marry a dentist once until his receptionist called her up and told her some things. She still thought of that one, how kind he was, how capable he looked in his white smock. After his receptionist called, though, and offered some confidential tips, funny things made more sense, how he wasn't always where he was supposed to be, how he was often late and jittery. But it tore her up getting loose from him. Still, Annie never stopped believing you should give everybody the benefit of the doubt.

"Rick," she said while yet again sitting on a railroad tie watching him work. Soon it would be too cold to sit out like this. "When are we going to combine our stuff in one place?" His apartment was dark and bare, to stay there long would make her feel like a prisoner.

"This is where I live; this is where I work."

"You could open your shop like I've been saying."

"Money's not pecans, it doesn't grow on trees," he said.

Annie thought Rick Nix could get a loan on his reputation as a mechanic. Hadn't he sold the Jaguar to a banker, and didn't that banker need Rick's help just to keep it on the road? Rick had told her as much, and now he saw why his daddy had warned him about bragging. "What somebody knows isn't worth a damn," he told Annie.

Once upon a time, what Rick Nix knew was worth something. Leonardo daVinci, Thomas Jefferson, you could bet guys like them would have been able to tune their own cars if they had them. When did we reach the point where there was too much to know? A world where little sacks of knowledge were stashed around here and there, not much use to anybody except the guy with lots of money? Nowadays, if you had money that was good enough; it got you the rest.

Rick Nix believed that, though he hadn't troubled to talk it out like a lot of other things. If he had, he might have said he was like one of those skinny, skinny trees he'd heard about in the Ouachita Mountains where his people had come from down into Texas. It turns out those little trees had been hanging on there for hundreds of years in that poor rocky dirt on top of mountains worn down to nubs. Regardless of how hard the wind blew, he'd be there when the morning came.

And Annie? She would always be after him about something, wouldn't she? If it wasn't his clothes, it was what he ate. Hey, he told her when he was in a good mood, he had been knocking around for over thirty years and hadn't gone naked or starved yet. When he was in a bad mood, he could act just like an old dog you're trying to take to the vet, get his head down, squint his eyes so all Annie could see was the heavy ridge of his eyebrows. You could try to drag him, but he would not be moved.

"If you think he's bad now," Barb said, "wait until he's sixty." But Annie said no, that he was just insecure. Love would soften him in time.

Probably she was right, probably Rick Nix could have been gentled into the kind of sweet husband any woman would want. Single men wake up in the morning and they're lonesome. That's when a good cup of coffee and a hug around the neck does them some good. That's why married men live longer instead of going out into the world mad every day. The trouble is, men don't know any of this.

Rick Nix started thinking of Annie around late afternoon, around supper time. That's when he would be cleaning up his tools with a little WD-40, covering the exposed engine of the Fiat Spyder he was working on with a plastic tarp, getting the grease from around his nails with an old toothbrush and some Go-Jo. That's when he wanted a good steak and a cold beer on the table. And afterwards, maybe with a movie or some TV in between to let that meat digest a little, he would pull Annie onto his lap and run his hand up under her skirt, inside her blouse. A little nooky on the couch or on her rug or in her bed, wherever, that was what he liked.

She would wake up at two in the morning to the sound of him zipping his pants, pulling his boots on with soft grunts. "What?"

"I want to get started early," he said and was gone.

In this way they stayed the same, but got to be farther apart. The old gas station on 38th and Lamar was bought and remodeled. Annie read in her own paper it was to be a dry cleaners. Rick bought and sold a half dozen cars including a red MG Midget. Annie wanted that one for herself; she hinted broadly, thinking Rick might give it to her, that giving it to her would prove he was committed. "You don't want it," he told her, "it's junk. Wait until something nice turns up." What and when would that be?

If Barb had been around, she would have told Annie this is not Shakespeare. No Robin Goodfellow with his quiver full of wobbly intentions is going to come along and help the tongue-tied and shy find words, goad the diffident and doubtful, soothe the petulant and brace up the wavering. You connect the dots all by yourself, kiddo. And with no help, they don't make a picture of a happy couple but of a bunch of lines that ought to have been connections.

Annie gave up. She accepted a date with the assistant managing editor of the paper, a guy with a too-neat mustache who had been after her for some time. It turned out he understood perfectly what a woman like

Annie could do for him, and so he dumped all his complaints and inse-
curities and needs on her. After a while, after they had been married for
a while, he would wring her good nature right out of her. Her nose would
seem to get more pointed, her chin more pronounced. Nobody would
cross Annie then, she'd fly all over them.

———————————

It's never really winter in Texas, not the kind of winter you see Yankees
having on TV when everybody's car is stuck in snowbanks and huffing
and puffing people in overcoats are out there pushing like mad. What
for? Where do they think they're going?

In Texas there are some winter days that will almost pass for spring.
The sun is bright enough to take the chill out of the wind, the birds that
have hung around get up in the morning and try to make a little noise.
On one of these days Rick Nix took a notion to take the car he was working on, a Jensen-Healy, out into the hill country for a drive. Ordinarily
he didn't drive the cars very much. He didn't want to run the mileage
up, and besides, most of them weren't any fun. This one was a little different; it had an American engine in it. Rick was feeling a little lonely
these days, even if he wouldn't admit it.

When Annie told him she was going to start dating the guy from her
newspaper, he wasn't surprised. They always leave you when they find
somebody better, he thought. It was a crazy thought, a mess of paranoid
and inferior feelings he had been cultivating all his life, and it could only
cause him to behave badly. He considered calling out that paper boy and
beating his ass, but these days that would only get him up on assault
charges. He thought about leaving hateful messages on Annie's machine,
but she had turned it off to avoid answering people's calls about Rick's
cars. So he took high-speed drives in the country instead.

He had turned right on 620 heading out of Bee Caves but hadn't
thought much about where that road would take him until he crossed
the dam. The lake stretched out to his left; it wasn't far to the turnoff
for Windy Point. When he came to the turn, he took it and turned into
the Oasis. Maybe what he needed was a beer. On the deck, Rick Nix felt

the wind blowing up from the lake; it was cooler than in town. Other people, couples mostly, were outside too, sitting in the few plastic chairs around the tables the help had unstacked. He took his beer and went to the railing.

Out in the lake, just behind the dam, was a big gray crescent like a lopsided half-moon. Rick Nix grabbed a waitress by the arm and said, "What's that out in the lake? What is that? I've never seen it before."

She stepped away from Rick; there was something scary about him just then, and she looked at the lake to see what he could possibly mean. "Oh that? That's Sometimes Island; it's only out when they draw the lake down."

"Damn," said Rick Nix. That Gibson was right. And now he was going to be rich. The guy was off to work in the oil business, a guy who didn't know oil when you showed it to him on his dipstick. That had been Rick's only other encounter with Gibson; he'd turned up and asked Rick to tune his car so he could sell it. He admitted it was junk before Rick could tell him, but thought maybe he would make more selling it if it ran smoother. But Gibson did not tell Rick Nix that Barb dumped him, that he was quitting school and taking off. Annie told him that, Annie who told him Gibson was sweet and that he should be more tolerant. Looking out onto the chilly lake, he considered how to do this: to open up his heart and be more tolerant.

Rick Nix thought of that boy down on Windy Point way back in the summer. Where would he be now? In school somewhere taking classes but not seeing the point of his studies, or enlisted, or working in a car-parts place. It didn't much matter; Rick could pretty much guess where to find him. In one of those cinder-block juke joints with a pool table and some video games. Sitting around a table with a bunch of other guys looking for something to fight over.

Rick Nix was too old for that sort of thing now. He would get over Annie, if getting over meant he would stop being mad. Then again he would never get over her. He would never get over her in the same way he could never get over his white Impala, his Jaguar, his high school girl. The things he had cared about, loved maybe, though it's hard to say if that's the word Rick would pick, all of them had gotten away from him. When did you come to the place where you got tired of fooling with wanting?

Annie could never guess how hard it was for Rick Nix. She could never know what it was like to want and want and want and never really have. It made you mad. Rick Nix's daddy sold his big white Chevy Impala when Rick was away in the service, traded it actually for a pickup truck and a horse trailer. And when Rick came home on leave and pitched a fit, the old man said, "Hell son, it wasn't but a Chevrolet." Rick Nix could still hear it. He would never be able to keep the things that came his way that were worth hanging onto; wasn't it best to just let the one go and look for another?

Rick Nix thought about asking the waitress out, but he saw he'd screwed that up. He went out to the low green car, unfastened the top and put it down. It was getting on towards dark; the wind would have a little more bite to it, but he wanted to feel it. He put the car in first and drove slowly from the parking lot to the main road.

When he came to the stop sign, he took a left. Now, where would he be headed? Up the road to a time when he would turn into mean old Uncle Rick, the relative his sisters and girl cousins argued about come holidays. Who would get stuck with having him over? Who, when he'd gotten so bad with his drinking and when he got drunk, would be so snappish with the children? Like the Christmas he had his broken ankle, broken when a car fell off the jack stand. Drunk when that happened probably, he had laid in the living room on the couch, trying to trip the kids with his crutches when they went running through the house playing with their toys.

What, his sisters would always wonder, could you do with a man like that? And where did he get off acting like that anyhow?

Ray's Boat

Ray looked down the dinner table at his assembled friends. Sitting with their chairs pushed back, a coffee cup resting here and there on a knee, they looked the very picture of satisfaction, maybe even bliss. On the table, the casserole dish was almost empty of its bricks of lasagna; the sticks of bread smeared with butter were all gone. So was the salad, so was the wine from the big two-liter bottles. There was still some cheesecake left. Somebody might still want another piece of that.

Ray looked on the flushed faces, the distended bellies of his guests, and thought everybody should eat like this. The world's leaders ought to be brought together and made to eat Sherri's wonderful lasagna. With so much blood tied up in the digestive track, the world could be made a safer place. He called for a toast. Nobody had any wine, but they had their water glasses and their coffee mugs, and with some effort they pulled themselves toward the center of the long table. Ray smiled. This disparate bunch overcame their drowsy inertia for him because they were his dear friends. "To this green world," he told them.

Nobody asked what his toast was all about. On this summer's evening when the trees, the grass, the lettuce and spinach in Sherri's garden threatened to push through the newly installed bay window right on into the dining room, people might have thought they understood him well enough. Besides, Ray was known by his toasts.

At one memorable dinner he had toasted, "To socks with no holes."

They ate that one on a partially refinished door straddled across a couple of sawhorses. They ate surrounded by buckets of paint and ladders and Ray's saws and hammers and drills. Then, only Ray had a sense of how his old house was going to come together or had the confidence that he and Sherri would reach a point when they could stop camping out in their underheated bedroom, could stop buying black beans and lentils in fifty-pound sacks at the feed store.

Ray's sock toast had marked the day when he would stop augmenting his wardrobe from stray articles of clothing picked up off the roadway. Back then when he rode his bicycle to work, he told people, he saw a wealth of things left to rot on the shoulder. T-shirts, knit hats, socks, gloves. Sometimes even pants and underwear. Once he found two brassieres left on a picnic table in a park, but Sherri wouldn't wear them. Surely, she said, there were limits.

But if there were such limits, Ray could never comprehend them. Now, with his house wrapped around him, newly plumbed, painted, and furnished, proof that he really had peeked into a brighter future, who could deny that he wasn't some kind of visionary?

Eight-thirty—people would have to start packing it in soon. Ray was thirty-one, most of his friends were about that. Their kids were somewhere along the route from diapers to preschool. Little ones were going to start falling apart in the next half hour. No more of that 2 A.M. shit, no more sitting around listening to Ray's tapes and talking. No more getting a little high.

"Wait," Ray said, "I got to show you what I found today."

Today, as he went to his job as foreman of a small crew of carpenters and painters who specialized in repairs to two-hundred-year-old houses, repairs for people who wanted only the best and could afford it; today, in his good-as-new pickup that he'd fixed up himself; today, Ray saw this guy dragging a big canvas bag out to the curb for the trash men to pick up. He wheeled over and asked what, exactly, that sack was all about.

"Junk," the guy said, "crap. You don't even want to hear about it."

"Well," Ray said, "I could take it if all you're going to do is send it to the dump." And the guy was more than happy to give him the bag and oddly shaped boards and bent steel rods, all the paraphernalia that went with it. All of it was piled in a heap in Ray's garage right now.

The men excused themselves from the table and poured the rest of the coffee into their mugs on the way out. After promising they wouldn't be long, they headed downstairs to the garage. But kids had already broken out of the bedroom with weary tears and recriminations. Ray's party was coming to a close and people would have to hurry to maintain this happy sense of equilibrium long enough to bathe their babies, put them to bed, and finally climb into bed themselves, where they would be free at last to share their built-up sense of well-being and love and of the rightness of their lives.

"Look at this," Ray said. The canvas fabric of the boat itself was already spread on the floor, looking like the flayed hide of a strange animal. He picked up two pieces of wood and slid them into a metal sleeve, twisted, and—ta da!—instant oar. "If the rest was this simple," he said in a make-believe mournful voice.

But by then men were taking up the various wooden shapes and turning them over in their hands, saying to each other: "This must be the transom, and that thing maybe will unfold and make the keel." "These steel hickeys must be the ribbing." Ray had, of course, already seen that much of the design, but it pleased him to watch his friends make it take shape.

By placing the steel rods through a double thick length of canvas webbing, the men began to assemble a ribbed backbone for some prehistoric lizard. The side door to the garage cracked open and a child's face looked in, not Ray's kid but another. "Mommy says," the girl started, but it was at that moment that Ray held up the skeleton and hollered out, "Looks like a whale! How'd you like to wind up in the belly of this thing?" The child scampered back up the stairs to the dining room.

With some pushing, the men were able to get the transom to pop into the stern of the boat skin. But that's when they lost Chuck, which was too bad since Chuck was a sculptor who was selling pretty well these days now that he'd gotten into a gallery in Richmond and one in D.C. too. Once he and Ray had put up flimsy apartment buildings together. "How are we going to finish this thing without him?" Ray said. "I mean, we need somebody whose brain works in 3-D."

But Chuck left anyway with his wife the printmaker and their bawling kid who'd overshot her bedtime and gone hyperactive on them. "I hate it when that happens," Ray told Len and Terry who were left, who had figured out the steel ribs weren't in the right order to fit into the slots along the canvas gunwales of the boat. "Great, terrific," Ray yelled at them, only now he saw that the canvas strip that held the ribs maybe should have gone in before the transom if the keel was to help stretch it the length of the boat.

His own child appeared at the door. "What is it, princess?" he asked her. With her long blonde hair and her ballerina tights, Bonnie really did look like a princess from one of her own storybooks. She whispered in his ear, "Mommy says it's past our bedtimes."

"Uh-oh, it's past our bedtimes," Ray told his pals.

"Oh man, you aren't kidding," said Len, who went to high school with Ray but got a law degree and turned into a Republican. Which goes to show, Ray thought, that life's a pretty crooked road. Take Terry, who sold a little dope, played drums in a country band. Who knows what all he did to pay the bills? But here he was in Ray's garage with Len.

Not for long. Len and Terry left. Ray heard the good-byes and the front door shut, maybe he could even hear Sherri throw the dead bolt. Alone, then, he sat on the floor and considered how the slim metal battens must fan out in some sort of umbrella fashion to make the bow.

Nobody had time for fun anymore. Now it was day-care, now it was deals. Real life, Ray's pals were fond of saying, had snuck up on them. Caught in house payments and car repairs, the shit they pledged themselves against not so long ago, not one of them would say it was a mistake. Like insects, they'd simply gone through a fast and unimagined alteration from larva to adult. Nobody even had a chance to say, "Now what?"

Ray and Sherri had two kids. Anybody could see Bonnie was daddy's girl. Ted was still a tiny baby in diapers so it was hard to say for sure, but Ray and Sherri worried about him. Ray's mom, if she was still alive, would say Ted wasn't right.

Ray sat on the floor, slapping a metal stay against his shin. Not right in what way? So far nobody could say. Sherri seemed to worry more about it than the doctor did. Ray listened for the noises his house ought to make. The ventilation fan in the attic ought to be shutting down about now if the thermostat he put in was working. Bonnie had been so quick to learn everything. Maybe Ted was just slow. Hell, Einstein was slow; there was nothing wrong with being slow.

They'd figure it out; put enough heads together and you can solve just about any problem. That's what Ray thought. Ted would turn out OK, just like the boat. Ray considered his boat a marvel. Sure, he still needed to do some fiddling with the ribs and patch a couple of holes that had been poked in the canvas hull. Above him, he could hear the drumming of Bonnie's feet as she ran from the tub to her bedroom and Sherri's heavier step following.

Ray's house didn't grow quiet. Directly above him in the kitchen, Ray could hear Sherri banging pots, running water and abruptly shutting it off. The rhythm of her movements alarmed him. Whenever something pissed her off, it always caught him by surprise.

Ted had been slow sitting up. They'd sit him on his rear and he'd just topple over like those sock-em toys Ray had as a boy. Only Ted didn't roll right back up. He was slow crawling, and now he was only walking clumsily, hanging on his mom's leg, not talking at all. Bonnie, though. Bonnie was a lucky girl. She was just like Ray. When he was a kid with a big dopey grin, strangers at the grocery store would fish in their pockets for pennies so he could work the gum machine. He knew doors would spring open for Bonnie the rest of her life; all she had to do was smile.

Ray made a list of stuff he needed to pick up from the shop or buy at the hardware to fix his new boat and went back up to the kitchen. He was surprised at the carnage left there. Red sauce ran down the cabinet fronts, a cone of coffee grounds spilled over the counter. Plates were piled in high crooked stacks. When Sherri turned around from the sink she was crying.

"Hey, hey," Ray told her. "That's what we got a dishwasher for, right?" Except Ray hadn't allowed for enough of a slope in the drain pipe, and it tended to get stopped up. It just had in the middle of running a load of pots and pans, and had disgorged itself all over the floor.

"You're no help," she told him. But he was. He was like the god-damned Cat in the Hat, charging into her kitchen, more a force like weather than any kind of human being. Whenever he pitched in, things ran wildly out of control. Dishes slid out of the over-filled drying rack, silverware went crashing, water sprayed across the room and hit the new wallpaper in the breakfast nook.

Now he was on his knees feeding a plumber's snake into the dishwasher. Sherri said, "You know how Ted is if you don't get him settled down." She said, "You know what it's like to get Bonnie her bath and get him put down at the same time." He knew, he knew. Maybe she was losing her delight in his disorder. Before the kids, her placid days at the county library could use an infusion of Ray's wacky attacks.

Ted started hollering from his bedroom. Poor little guy would be waking up this way throughout the night now, sweating, rolling his big blue eyes around. Nightmares might be what it was, and him not even able to tell them about it.

When, exactly, was it that Sherri saw she was getting tired of Ray? When was it that she began to realize that one of the reasons she could stay on at the library year after year when nothing ever changed, when it was the same work of being quietly pleasant every day, was Ray? He was like a radio turned up way too loud, but locked a room away and out of reach.

When he got her on the phone, the sound of a power tool whirring in the background, he never apologized for not being where he said he would be. "Ray, we're supposed to be taking the kids to the pool," she said.

"No problem. I'll meet you there in the truck. Pack me a couple of sandwiches—ham, mustard and mayonnaise."

"Ray," Sherri could say, but the phone would already be dead so there was no chance to explain that the kids were already in their swimsuits, Ted was in his car seat bellowing, and she would have to stop for gas too since he left her with an empty tank.

Whenever Sherri thought of Dr. Roger Armstead, she thought of a big brown dress shoe, worn over in the heel, a hole in the sole, scuffed, with a broken and knotted shoelace. He was a big man, six-three or -four with long brown hair shot with gray and a thick gray beard. Every day he wore wrinkled and stained khaki pants, a light blue dress shirt, also wrinkled even if he put it on fresh in the morning, and a blue and orange striped tie. The man was her boss at the library and from the beginning she found him mildly repulsive. How was it she agreed to have lunch with Dr. Roger Armstead?

Dr. Roger was what he liked to be called, and everybody at the library knew a version of his story. Once he was a history professor at UVA, but they let him go. Maybe it was for drinking, maybe it was for not doing his work or hitting on coeds. Whatever, they let him go. His family, though, was rich; his family went way back in Virginia history. Probably they lent Thomas Jefferson money once. So Dr. Roger came to be director of this small branch of the Albermarle County Library, which was OK since it wasn't a real library and since there were enough people who knew what was what to take up the slack. Meanwhile, Dr. Roger spent his days arguing about history and politics with some of the old men patrons who didn't seem to mind his lax personal hygiene.

Knowing what she knew, Sherri went to lunch with Dr. Roger Armstead at the all-you-can-eat Chinese buffet place. "How is Raymond?" he asked her, and "How is pretty little Bonnie?" and "How is Ted coming along? Are you still worried about him?" Sherri answered these questions while she felt like she was having a lucid dream. One part of her mind was sour and alert and told her this man probably had to sneak around that very morning and ask the other librarians the names of her husband and kids, that his was a clever act, assembling his next thoughtful question out of the clues from Sherri's previous answer. An ex-bullshitting professor. But another part said, that's OK, relax, you need this. You need to sit down and talk to somebody about yourself. And it felt good that somebody was a man.

She agreed it would be fine to swing by his house and drop off some papers on the way back to work, telling herself she was curious to see if it was as messy and nasty as his office and the Oldsmobile they rode in. When they pulled into the drive of Dr. Roger's tall brick house, he rooted around in the rubble in the back seat until he found some yellowed papers in no way distinguishable from those he left behind. "Won't you come in?" There was another little voice in her head, the voice that was around from her excitable girlhood readings of Edgar Allan Poe and H.P. Lovecraft, saying, *Don't open that door, don't go down that hallway.* Her more adult voice, the voice of a librarian and mother of two, said, *Don't be so silly.*

The house was, in fact, messier and smelled like a dirty man, a little like sweat, a little like pee. Stacks of old newspapers and magazines slid from every flat surface down into the middle of the floor. "My research," said Dr. Roger. Sherri wondered what sort of research he did, then she wondered how much of this material had been carried off from their very library without authorization. Underneath the papers and the dust was fine old cherry furniture and oriental rugs too. These had been worth something before the moths got after them. Maybe the furniture still was. Back in the kitchen, Dr. Roger could be heard making them drinks.

"How about a gin and tonic?" he hollered. Sherri walked in the direction of his voice. "Oh, oh you shouldn't have come in here." Dr. Roger's kitchen had been white once, but now it was yellow with a fine patina of fuzzy dust hanging to the greasy walls. The enamel around the eyes on his stove had grown tentacles of grimy rust and his sink was brown. "My mother was a saintly woman," Dr. Roger told her. "I keep this house out of respect for her memory."

In this way he mocked his sloth and made Sherri feel sorry for him while at the same time she knew he was trying in his clumsy way to seduce her. She found herself oddly grateful for the effort and accepted his offer of the drink, though she rarely drank liquor at all.

Loving Ray would be enough to wear anybody out. He turned each day into an obstacle course, not so much to be got over and around, but to be knocked down. Even Sunday began with the whine of a power tool. Maybe he was putting in a new window sash, or a new radiator in his truck, or building a jungle gym for the kids. Whatever, he ran from job to job, and none of them ever quite got done. The radiator might wind up fully installed but lacking a thermostat, so for a week he would have to take the station wagon to work until he found the time to stop at the car parts place. The window sash never got painted, and the jungle gym remained an odd assortment of four-by-four posts standing in the backyard.

"Think of it as a temple," he told Sherri, "like Stonehenge. On the first day of summer the sun is going to come up and sit right on top of that post." He ran over to the post and rested his chin on top.

"Don't be silly, Ray," she told him, and from behind her Bonnie on her powder blue tricycle said, "Don't be silly, Daddy."

It would be wrong to think these projects had been forgotten. In Ray's mind, his work was always in evolution. Part of his brain scanned his basement and garage inventory for the bolts he bought for the jungle gym and the weights for the window sash he'd salvaged from a fire damaged house. In the middle of the night Sherri would wake up to the light in her eyes while he wrote notes to himself, sketched ideas on the pad he kept beside their bed.

"There's a million ways to get things done, a million ways to make things work out," Ray sang to himself while he carefully, carefully worked his pry bar under a dry rotted floor joist. The trick was to take out the joists one at a time and replace them without damaging the floor above. Ray liked his work and didn't especially mind being chief since everybody on his crew was a pretty good worker. Except the new guy. All day Ray had been thinking about the new guy. For one thing, nobody was sure what the new guy did. He wasn't a carpenter; he wasn't really a painter, though he claimed to be.

Ray would come up from under the house and find this guy, Dave, sitting on the ground smoking, gazing at the windowsill he was supposed to be scraping, sanding and caulking like it was one of life's bigger mysteries. "Hey," he'd say, "just taking a little break. What's up?" It occurred to Ray that since it looked like he himself was taking a break maybe Dave thought taking breaks was OK. And it was, everybody took a five-minute break in the morning and in the afternoon. But somehow Ray knew this guy's breaks ran longer.

"Maybe I could see if anybody wants a Coke or something," Dave said thoughtfully.

Ray found some money in his pocket for a soda and told Dave to go around and see if anybody else wanted something from the store before he went. Shortly he heard Dave gunning the engine in the company van and remembered Dave wasn't supposed to be driving. His license had been revoked.

One of the painters came around the house. "We got to talk about that guy," he told Ray.

"I know, I know. What do you want me to do?"

"Tell the bosses. Tell the bosses to fire him."

The bosses. Ray tried to stay away from the bosses as much as he could. They bid the jobs, got the contracts. As long as Ray's crew brought the jobs in on estimate, they stayed away. Everybody on all the crews was happier that way.

Occasionally a boss came by driving one of the green Chevy station wagons that matched the green Ford vans the crews used. All of them had the company name printed discreetly on the side. On a good day, Ray liked to imagine Charlottesville being crisscrossed all day long by the station wagons and vans—stitching it back together through careful, crafty workmanship. Two-hundred-year-old houses don't stand up all by themselves. On a bad day, Ray thought of the green vehicles as locusts or alien invaders, taking over the world silently, sneakily unless somebody woke up and noticed.

He got that feeling sitting in the air-conditioned seat, a gallon of newly tinted paint between his feet, listening to a boss bitch him out about a guy on his crew who wasn't shaving every day, or about eating their lunch under the big oaks in a client's front yard. All the time, the radio softly bleated, "Jesus, Jesus, Jesus," since the bosses always tuned to the religious station. Taking over the world through niceness and neatness, Ray thought.

Dave was tight with the bosses. They hired him through the pastor at their church who found him while sharing a moment of prayer at a minimum security prison. When he came to work, he had no brushes of his own and wore a black T-shirt featuring the name of a rock band and a large cannabis leaf. His clothes, the bosses said, were leftovers from his former life and, just now, were the only ones he had. Praise Jesus for the gift of Dave's repentance.

God's world is full of such miracles, the bosses would tell you if they thought you were worthy of sharing their insiders' knowledge. One by one they had been converted from Sunday golfers to acolytes of a true faith, though they were still a little cagey about revealing their clean new souls to prospective clients. This they professed to believe: The world as we know it is coming to an end right around the corner, and in its place a new heaven on earth will be established for a chosen few. Wondrously, that new heaven would resemble the rolling Virginia piedmont with each hilltop crowned by a red brick mansion, the countryside scourged of strip malls, condo developments, trailer homes, and plywood minibarns. It would look rather like the Old Virginia of Mr. Jefferson's time had he only been their kind of God-fearing man.

On her way home Sherri stopped at a convenience store and bought some breath mints. She really had nothing to hide; she just didn't want to have to explain to Ray all the things she had seen and heard. Dr. Roger's cannonball, for example, a real Civil War cannonball he had dug out of a pasture in Manassas. There's probably a law against that now, she thought. There was probably a law against it then. But since Dr. Roger's family had entertained Major Mosby right in the room where she was sitting, Dr. Roger felt that gave him the right.

It seems he came from a long line of people who felt they had certain special rights. His father had been a judge, and his grandfather before that, and to hear Dr. Roger tell it, they had devoted their legal lives to pushing the unwashed back from the breastworks. He winked so Sherri, up from Nelson County with two years at the community college, understood she was one who slipped through. "It's nothing to be ashamed of," Dr. Roger told her.

Until she and Ray moved into town, she had never imagined it was. She told Dr. Roger her own family had fought in the War Between the States.

"On which side?"

"The Rebel side, of course," she said, suddenly feeling proud over something that hadn't meant that much to her before.

"They were fools, then, weren't they?" Dr. Roger said. He said Johnny Reb died defending an institution that held nothing for him. He had been tricked because he loved the land too much. You shouldn't love anything that much, Dr. Roger told her.

He had made his own life a monument to indifference. He had shambled through the same University of Virginia where his family had previously distinguished itself and then been drummed out of the law school after representing the work of another Virginia gentleman as his own. His old man pulled some strings to get Dr. Roger instated in the graduate school of a neighboring state university so he might come home to teach in a position created just for him. In the same manner he spilled his corn flakes onto the kitchen floor, clipped his nails over the fine carpets in the sitting room, he had pissed his sinecure away.

"Your poor momma and daddy," Sherri said. She wasn't sure if it was the right thing to say or not. It just came out.

Dr. Roger just smiled, "Oh hell, he didn't care about me."

"Your mother, then." Sherri had the notion women could be counted on to love people more than ideas or things.

"Yes, Mother." Dr. Roger cocked his head and looked into her face, blinking his big old eyes.

Sherri thought it was time to be getting back to the library.

Nothing had happened, had it? Except Sherri knew even as she walked back into the warm sunshine from Dr. Roger's musty house she would mention none of it to Ray. The way he was, and he really couldn't help it, you couldn't keep anything to yourself. He had to be poking into everything.

―――――――――

When Sherri drove up from picking up Bonnie at her dance class and Ted from day care, Ray was sitting in the open door of his truck reading. "Who can find a virtuous woman? For her price is above rubies," he told her.

Sherri blushed, but Ray had his nose in the book and didn't notice. "Ray, what are you talking about?" She could hear her voice bouncing around inside her head like she was listening to herself on a tape recorder.

He held up a green pocket Bible about the size of a deck of cards. Dave had given it to him; Dave had given one to everybody on the crew that morning while they were riding the van out to Farmington. Guys who were used to purposefully taking up all manner of tools held the pocket testaments nervously, tenderly, then put them away in their shirt pockets or dinner buckets. Nobody said anything.

Just as they pulled into the driveway of a pre-Civil War manor house in need of minor sprucing up, Dave spoke. "I'm wondering if anybody might want to join me in a moment of prayer?" Everybody sat real still, but they were all looking at Ray. Another carpenter, the guy riding shotgun, said, "No," and got out and slammed the door.

Ray said, "Well, Dave, I guess we all have our own ways of getting ready for work."

"Huh." And all day Dave sulked around, doing even less than he usually did. At lunch he went to the back of the large yard and ate by himself.

What could you do with a guy like that? Ray had nothing against Jesus, but work was work. Still, the little green Bible was a kick. He took it out at lunchtime and started at the beginning with old God himself rolling his voice out on the waters. He started reading slowly in a deep, serious voice, "In the beginning," but everybody told him to put a sock in it. "No kidding," Ray said, "we could start reading to each other at lunchtime. Not just this," though he thought to himself he liked the sound of the Bible, its rhythms reached back to his kid days and put him at ease, "but Louis L'Amour books and detective stories, you know?"

They didn't know. And neither did Ray. Not really. Now that his house was pretty much finished, now that his imagination had some time to run loose, he was wondering, what else was there?

"You know what I mean?" he said to Len. They met for breakfast once a week before they went off to their different jobs, and they were both pleased about the impression they made: Ray in his carpenter's jeans and dirty ball cap, Len in his slick suit. They must be special people to be such friends.

But Len didn't know. The law, he thought, was a wonder in itself. Every time you thought you got to the end of some problem, it seemed like you went down a trap door into a whole new way of thinking. It was all words, all the way you put together words, all different every day.

"Well, sure," said Ray, "that's just like a house. You're never really done, there's always something else. But I mean something different. Something that isn't a house or the law. Something else."

Len said maybe there wasn't anything else.

"Even in the woods?"

"Even in the woods."

"Even in the woods with your hands in your pockets and you not thinking about cutting down a tree you're not supposed to or catching a fish out of season or pissing and having somebody accidentally see you?"

Len said no.

Ray said, "Maybe there's a way of thinking that just doesn't have anything to do with the law."

Len said, "That would be chaos." He said our social fabric was thin as ten-cent toilet paper, and without the law there we would fall right through it. And he picked up his greasy napkin and poked a hole in it so Ray would see.

"No kidding?" Ray said. "You believe that?" Then he said they should go fishing for smallmouth bass in his new boat, and Len agreed they should do just that. The question was when. Len was busy all the time these days, even on weekends. Still, it had been a long time since they went fishing together, since either of them had gone fishing at all. As soon as Ray finished the boat, maybe they really would.

Sherri said she'd hate to be married to that guy. Which surprised her. She used to think Len was cute, sly and sexy. Back then he put words together in ways that made you laugh. Now he sat at the table with his hands made into a church steeple and lined his nose up at you like he was taking a bead: one false move and blam-o. Len's life seemed like it had turned into a big argument, and he had to win it.

"I'm glad you're not like that," she told Ray and meant it. She was still feeling bad about eating Chinese food with Dr. Roger. Besides, it gave her gas. Maybe they would have steaks for dinner. They weren't good for you, even Ray agreed with that, but he still liked them, and eating a steak made him feel like he had amounted to something.

"I bet Len has steaks all the time," Ray told her.

No, Sherri said, they took casseroles and stuff out of the freezer and nuked them. Len's wife was a lawyer too. They had one kid, a prissy little boy with a real big head. He was already reading on the fifth-grade level, and he was just in preschool.

"Well, Bonnie's prettier, aren't you honey?" Ray said.

"He's dweeby," Bonnie said.

"Ted now." Ray took Ted out of the car seat and swung him up over his head, down between his legs, threw him a couple of feet in the air, and caught him.

"Ray!"

"It's OK. I'm getting him ready for a future in outer space." He pulled Ted's face up to his own. "Right, buddy? You thinking your deep thoughts in there? You happy?"

Ted giggled and snorted.

"See? He's all right. He just doesn't have any complaints."

Nonetheless, Sherri insisted they make an appointment for Ted at

University Hospital. In Nelson County when they were kids, you went to the doc when you were sick, and that was that. People grew up the way they grew up, and that was that. You loved them anyway. Maybe, Ray thought, some old ways were better.

————————

Ray's crew knocked off, gathered up their tools, and headed for the van. The smell of marijuana rolled out its doors. Everybody looked at Dave; Dave sniggered. Work was getting to be this way, a series of little trials for Ray.

On the way back to the shop, nobody said anything. Then one of the guys said, "I don't know about you, but I need this job."

"I kind of like a job," somebody else said. They were all looking at Ray now except for Dave, who was slid over by the cracked open window letting the wind blow over him, looking like he was all blissed out.

"OK, OK," Ray said, "everybody who needs a job hold up your hand." They all did, even Dave.

"Good. That's settled." And he drove on.

Terry knew Dave. Only he called him Crazy Dave. Crazy Dave used to hang out with the garage bands that played for frat parties over at the U, a kind of roadie for bands that never got to go on the road. Shit-faced every time you saw him.

"Was he any good at it?" Ray wondered. He was still hoping Dave might turn out to be good at something.

"What's to be good at? You run around with a roll of duct tape and make sure all the equipment is plugged in. Somebody who knows a little bit runs the sound board." But Terry didn't know Dave had been in jail or found Jesus in there. It figured, though, Jesus or Buddha or somebody like that. He would be the type.

Ray showed Terry the little Bible Dave gave him. "I've been reading in it a little."

"You can pick those things up all over the place—the jails, the detox places, soup kitchens. They're always trying to get you when you're down."

"I kind of like the Old Testament part."

"You better get rid of that guy," Terry told him.

"You think so?"

"Fire him, Ray. Christ, you've fired people before, right?"

But Ray never had. He always just let things in the crew roll along until they sorted themselves out somehow. "Listen, I nearly got my boat finished. Let's you and me and Len go fishing."

"Ray."

"I'll talk to him."

But he kept putting it off. There was Dave, still eating lunch by himself, out under a huge old oak tree, studying his own scuffed up little Bible. What if—and this was what was really bugging Ray—what if this guy was really onto something? Here were these Children of Israel always getting it wrong, following false prophets, worshipping golden calves; you could bet they'd miss the genuine article when it came along. Across the yard, Dave chewed a big hunk off his sandwich, grinned, and wagged his head just like he knew what Ray was thinking.

After dinner Ray told Sherri he wanted to work on his boat, but really all he wanted to do was go sit in the garage and look at it. Ray thought his boat a wonder. A hybrid of umbrella and bicycle, it only looked complicated until you got used to it. Now all its ribs were ordered in their webbed canvas spine, and he had solved the problem of the folding wooden keel. Driving home from work one day, Ray saw how it would work. It was just a matter of opening the keel on its hinges over the top of the canvas spine and locking it against the transom and the point of the bow where the metal battens fanned out. All put together, Ray's boat had an optimistic sense of motion. He saw it was a miracle of design. Steel, canvas and wood, the reliable old materials of the mechanical age. You look at them every day, and one day you see how they could be made into a collapsible boat. Some clever guy, somebody a lot like Ray, had thought of this boat. All it needed now was painting.

Upstairs he could hear Sherri doing the dishes, his job. Tonight she was cutting him some slack, probably because she had been on his case so much about Ted. He thought he wanted to explain to her about Ted, about just giving him some time. But really what he wanted to do was explain to her about himself. Inside him, strangely shaped notions were growing. He could quit work and ride a bicycle across the country, for example, or build a small airplane in the backyard, then circle the globe in it. A little voice kept telling him to go do it and find out.

The door bumped open and Bonnie came in carrying Ted.

"Honey, you aren't supposed to be carrying him around like that; you'll hurt yourself. Him too. Put him down so he'll walk."

"It's OK, I do it all the time. You just never see me." She leaned against him and looked at the boat. "That's a silly boat. I wouldn't ride in a boat like that."

"What are you talking about?" Ray said. "This is a great boat. This is a magic boat, a boat that goes in a bag."

"Mommy says it's rotten junk, and you're stupid if you think you can make something out of it."

He was going to tell her how little Mommy knew about it when Ted, who was pulling himself around the room by holding to the walls and shelves, grabbed hold of the stubby cord to Ray's Skilsaw. Ray hollered, "Ted!" and in two big steps grabbed the saw just as it slid from its shelf. Ted looked at him, but it was a blank look, a look that registered neither panic nor fear.

"Take him out of here," Ray told Bonnie. "This isn't a place for little guys. This isn't a place for fooling around."

In a house full of the sounds of hammers and saws and drills, couldn't the sound of Ray's voice be one more noisy thing? He and Sherri never hollered at each other, even when they argued. Still, when was a voice a voice and not just another noise?

Ray decided right then he would paint his boat green. He took down a can of green enamel porch paint, opened it, and carefully stirred. He saw that he had been saving this quart of paint for a job just like this. Ordinarily he didn't like to paint; that's what God made painters for. But sliding the fresh bright paint over the canvas hull, pulling a river of green with his brush, and covering up the dirty brown, Ray was seeing the boat make itself new. Maybe everything was still possible, he couldn't be wrong about something big like that. Ray's boat was ready for some river or lake, some new place he had never explored. Ray was ready too. He and Len and Terry were going to fish in this boat; they had all promised.

———————

There was something needful about Dr. Roger that people never saw around the library, where he could be high-handed and mean to the patrons. Away from the building, he could sometimes be courtly and shy. He was a fat middle-aged man. Maybe nobody had ever loved him. Not his daddy. Not his mother either, no matter what Dr. Roger thought. How could she have stood by and let him ruin himself like that if she did?

Dr. Roger started asking Sherri to go to the Chinese place every week. Sometimes she tried to get out of it; sometimes she tried to suggest some place different, but he wouldn't hear it. "All you can eat. Isn't that the American way, all you can eat?" Real Chinese places didn't serve Jell-O, she told him, and the next time they went he made a point of eating a bowl of red Jell-O. "Here, taste that and tell me whether it's strawberry or cherry. I can never tell the difference," Dr. Roger said, poking a wobbling cube on a spoon in her direction.

Was he making fun of her when he did this, or not? Sherri couldn't tell, but she knew she didn't like it, and she didn't like it when he called their lunches out of the library "dates." "I've got a date with Miz Sherri for lunch today," he told the other librarians in the morning, "so don't go getting your hopes up. My social calendar is filled."

Often he protracted their absence by making up specious errands. One day as they drove all the way downtown to pick up some special kind of pipe tobacco he said he could get only at this one little shop, they passed a young woman wearing white shorts and a sports bra riding a bicycle. Sherri watched Dr. Roger's eyes roll to the rearview mirror as they passed. "Look out," she told him when the car started to drift to the left. "Oh, oh," he told her. "There ought to be a law. They do that to indulge themselves, you know. To make fools out of old men like me."

"Who? Who's they?" She was only teasing, but Dr. Roger didn't say anything.

When he parked the car, he caught her looking at him in the mirror. "Sometimes you think you can trust somebody. You take them into your confidence, and they let you down." His voice got heavy and slow. "They betray you." He sighed a purposeful sigh. "Stay in the car; I'll only be a minute."

The trouble with Ray was that he could make everything he needed in his workshop. Hadn't he remanufactured his house right up around him? Where did Sherri come in? "You're a good cook; you're a good lay" was what he told her. He meant he loved her. And he would do anything for the kids. But what did he need from her? She thought he might disappear down into that workshop one day and get ahold of a project so big and complicated he might stay there forever.

When Dr. Roger came back, he made his voice sound cheerful and offered to buy her a drink.

Those stories she'd heard at the library about Dr. Roger and college girls must have been true. Like those girls who wore tight shorts on bicycles, Sherri was thinking, they knew what they were up to as much as he did. He hurt them; he took advantage. But he got hurt too.

"Don't you have any hobbies?" Sherri asked him.

When Ray cracked open the inner office door, he saw the bosses kneeling on the gray industrial carpeting, down on one knee like high school ballplayers in their pregame locker room. The secretary, who was like all the other secretaries he had known in construction outfits, a pretty young woman in a short skirt, tiptoed around them with the coffee makings. When she looked up and saw Ray, she made a violent chopping gesture. When he made to shut the door, she slipped out beside him.

She grabbed the tail of his T-shirt and twisted it into a knot. "Are you crazy?"

"What's going on in there?"

"What's it look like? Ray, you better get out of here; you're in trouble with them already."

But before he could pull out of the parking lot, one of the bosses hollered to him and came jogging toward the van. "Ray, what's your question?"

"Nothing. It was something, but I think I can get it worked out."

"Do you?" The boss's face was heavy and lined, the face of a guy who drank too much, who had a closet full of secret debts and family troubles. "We're praying for you, Ray."

It was good to work with a bunch of wise-asses, good to take the edge off. "Woo woo," they hollered as soon as the van rocked out of the parking lot, "We're praying for you too, Ray," and "Praise Jesus, He wants you for a sunbeam." Dave sat in the very back seat grinning. Seven-thirty in the morning, and was he out of his gourd already?

It was good, because Ray was feeling scared. Not of the bosses. They were assholes, as lost as he was; anybody could see that. Ray was scared of the wide world opening out on him in a way he had been too busy to notice before. Hadn't he always said there wasn't a problem anywhere the right combination of time and money couldn't fix? Ray knew he had been blessed with more time than money, but that was OK. He had just revised his estimation: Time and the right tools.

Now he considered that he just might be mistaken. People, for example. People could get in such a way they couldn't be fixed. He wasn't thinking about Ted or even Crazy Dave. He was thinking about Sherri, how she got to be the way she was. She had been at the library so long she was starting to see their whole life as a matter of neatness and keeping your voice down. A book on the wrong shelf was as good as a book lost, she told him. Which was maybe a good way to think of books, but he wanted to leave room for possibilities, to allow room for whatever he hadn't thought of yet. He was thinking that when he needed to talk to somebody he went to Len or Terry and not to her. But Len had his laws and was so balled up in them he couldn't see anything else. And Terry had his drums. When things got too bad for him, he just went out in the shed behind his house and wailed. An hour or so of that would mellow anybody out. A good example of time and the right tools, Ray thought.

He never stopped to consider what would happen when time and possibility worked against him. He could not picture the day when Sherri went back to Dr. Roger's house, this time going in with a bellyache and resignation to see his rare and famous Civil War sword. Dr. Roger kept it in his bottom dresser drawer under piles of black socks. "You can't go wrong with black socks," he told her, "just get up in the morning and grab a couple."

Sherri looked into the open door of Dr. Roger's closet full of rows of blue shirts on hangers and more thrown up on the shelves still in their shrink-wrap packaging. Beside them were four or five pairs of wrinkled pants. His bathrobe hung on the door with his slippers, those leather slip-ons she always associated with corny old cartoon variations on dogs, newspapers, and fetching, kicked off on the floor below.

This is how it was, then, with the bedclothes thrown back to show an elongated yellow stain the approximate shape of Dr. Roger running down the middle of the sheet; Dr. Roger's mother, a horsy intelligent woman, staring critically out of a tarnished silver frame from the dresser top; and Dr. Roger himself grunting to his feet with the long sword and scabbard in his hands. Sherri looked at the sword with tassels hanging from its basket. Once they had been golden, but now they were faded to a pale pea green. Dr. Roger offered the sword to her, and in reaching for it she saw in his face a look of greedy anticipation bordering on joy. Sherri burst into tears. Dr. Roger wrapped her in his damp, hairy arms and pulled her to him, the cold sword pushing against her bottom. They stood this way in the middle of his bedroom for some time while she cried and cried like Bonnie when she dumped over on her tricycle.

By high summer, stands of cumulus clouds twenty stories tall come rolling up from the tidewater and across the piedmont until they stack up against the Blue Ridge. By lunchtime it would already be humid enough to make Ray want to step out of his clothes and wring them out. By three o'clock the clouds would have packed and darkened, and Ray's crew would start to climb off their ladders and unplug their power tools and make ready to hop in the van and run back to the shop with the slapping wipers on high speed and still not able to keep up with the rain water rolling down the windshield. They passed people standing soaking at the bus stops, cars stalled out in intersections. All around them, water ran down the parking lots and roadways, into gutters and storm drains, down, down the shingles of the world, cleansing away the carbon monoxide and sulfur dioxide in the air, the spilled antifreeze and motor oil on the highway, the bird shit and corrosion from the statue of Lewis and Clark and their doughty men, carrying it all to the James, the Rapidan, the Rappahannock, those beautiful green rivers of Virginia where in their time Captains Meriwether and William were known to wet a line in the springtime.

How could they have guessed? How could Mr. Jefferson himself, sitting up in his big old cluttered house always in need of some work, the French doors thrown open to get a little air moving, sitting there puzzling over a mammoth tusk, how could he have known? Sending those two redoubtable country boys over hills and valleys to the westward would wind up making life hell for little fishes.

All of which set Ray to thinking about what you aim for and what you get. Right here at the stoplight where water ran off the bronze hats of Lewis and Clark and made them look like they had just walked up from the bottom of the ocean into this unexpected world. Take a right and you're at University Hospital, where doctors with wires, electrodes, and a ray gun were all set to tell him and Sherri what was going on inside Ted's little head.

"Not so smart," Ray said. He meant getting off the bypass and driving through town, but he might have meant something he just now only felt and could not say. He moved as a wheel inside a wheel, inside lots of bigger wheels. The kids, Sherri, the house—these were things he thought he had planned for and wanted, but maybe they were all part of a bigger kind of movement he couldn't see or understand, that he had no more planned for than he had budgeted time for day and night or space for land and water.

In the parking lot outside the shop, the guys on his crew threw open the van doors and ran like hell indoors or off to their cars. Crazy Dave crawled out like he had been napping back in his seat, stood in the rain stretching, pulled his T-shirt off, and turned his face up to the sky. After a while the rain slacked off and more light came back into the day. Dave started off slow and easy to his car, and Ray went after him.

Ray had been meaning to talk to Dave for some time, hadn't he? He had been planning to tell him to get off his ass and make an honest effort, to stay straight on the job and not bullshit him because there was a difference between how you handled yourself around the guys and how you handled yourself around the bosses. He needed to tell him to take some of his payday and buy his own brushes. Instead he said, "Thanks for the Bible."

"No problem," Dave told him as he started to climb in his sky-blue Pinto. Somebody from the bosses' church had given it to him; all he'd added was the stereo tape deck and the two carton-sized speakers leaning against the back seat.

"Hey," Ray said, "I've got this new boat. I've been thinking about taking it out and doing a little fishing."

"The old back-to-nature thing," Dave said, like he already knew all about it.

"Something like that." Ray felt like Dave was looking him over from his orange ball cap advertising his favorite brand of chain saws to his work boots spattered with wood glue and paint as if he'd seen him for the very first time. "What I mean is you might like to go."

Dave took out his cigarettes and shook the pack around, peeked into the hole torn in the corner, then reached in with one skinny finger and pulled out a one-guy joint hardly fatter than a pencil lead. Before he lit up, he took a little look around him. He pulled on the joint, then offered it to Ray. "Maybe," he said through the smoke leaking out of his mouth, "maybe I could." If Ray took a hit, it would hardly leave any for Dave, but taking it seemed like the right thing to do now. Dave grinned, "Jesus got into fishing too."

When Ray got to his truck, he felt a little like puking. A hit on an empty stomach will do that to you sometimes. But it was something else. For one thing, he'd promised Sherri he'd give up marijuana now that Bonnie was getting big enough to know. He rolled down both windows and turned the vent window in so it would blow straight at him. The streets were already steaming anyway, and the humidity was even higher than before the storm. No, Ray decided, it was that Dave guy. He wasn't sure he wanted him in his fishing boat, hadn't meant to ask him. But when the time came, nobody else could go fishing. Len, well Ray could have guessed how it would be with Len, the family thing, the billable hours at his practice. He said he had to protect his time. Terry's band had a gig at a club in Bethesda; this could be a big break for them. Ray thought he'd heard that one before, but never mind. He even called Chuck, who he hadn't seen since the night of his big dinner. Ray was embarrassed by that, but Chuck was busy anyway. His wife was having an opening at a new gallery in Baltimore. If it went well, they would drive over and dance to Terry's band afterwards.

By now, it was moving into fall, a drizzly day and a little cooler. There was an honest chance of getting some fish if you knew where to go. Ray thought he did if he could find the place, up in the mountains, a little green lake he had fished once as a boy, somewhere off the Blue Ridge Parkway. He put his collapsed boat in the back of his truck, put in his rods and reels, the same old stuff he and his daddy had used, cleaned and oiled up with new six-pound test line. He put Ted in his baby seat and Bonnie next to him.

Sherri had already made it clear she didn't want the kids to go. Even Bonnie was too little, she said. She said her say the night before, when Ray sprung the trip on her at the last minute the way he always did. Bonnie would do all right, Ray said; she'd do fine if he baited her hook and took her fish off for her.

A picture of Ray's fishing expedition formed in Sherri's head as an illustration from a children's book, the half-rotten skin of the boat wobbling like Jell-O under a little girl wearing a bright yellow slicker and a perplexed expression. A child who knew better, but didn't know how to say so. Like Jell-O, she thought, forgetting that once Ray's immunity to all things ridiculous had been a reason she loved him. In another picture, she saw the child in the swamped and sinking boat reaching out of the page, crying out. That child was Bonnie. "Why don't you take Ted too?" she told him.

"OK," he said. And she saw herself trapped by her own contrary impulse. Isn't that the way it always is? A fairy queen left waiting for all the ugly consequences she brought on herself?

So she stayed back in the bedroom, fretting and listening to Ray in the kitchen pouring Bonnie her Coco Puffs, feeding Ted his cream of wheat, crooning, "Would you like to swing on a star? Carry moonbeams home in a jar?" in that bouncy Ray voice designed both to put them at ease and excite them.

"It's raining, Daddy," Bonnie told him.

"That's all right. That's good. Fish like it when it rains; they don't mind getting caught so much."

"Oh," she said. Sherri could hear the doubt seeping out of her daughter's voice. And why not? Ray had been doing the same thing to her for years. With Ray, there was always a hitch, always something more than he let on. Just like that conniving Cat in the Hat, he came around talking about fun, but only made trouble.

He hadn't mentioned Crazy Dave. He hadn't mentioned that all four of them would ride in the cab, where there were only two retrofitted seat belts and a piece of nylon rope strung between to hold down the baby seat, or that Dave would smoke his Marlboros all the way up the mountain.

Sherri watched out the window as Ray got the kids and his gear loaded. Maybe he would take a step back and look at the truck and the boat and the weather, take a look at himself and what he was getting into, and just give it up, quit. But Ray had never done that; what made her think he'd do it now?

She made herself a pot of tea and put it in a quilted cozy shaped like a laying hen. Ray was right; this was what she always said she wanted to do. She went into the living room and looked at her little shelf of books. They didn't keep many books that weren't shop manuals. Why keep books when you work in a library full of them? was what Ray told her.

She took down *Wuthering Heights*, the kind of book she thought she ought to read on a dreary day, wrapped up with a quilt and a cup of tea. But did she really want Heathcliff coming into her house, in his muddy boots, dripping with rain and smelling of sex? She walked around all the rooms and looked out the windows, hoping to be surprised by a different view. Then she put on her raincoat and got in her station wagon; maybe she would go shopping or just go for a drive.

There were parts of Charlottesville Ray didn't know about. Crazy Dave lived in one, toward downtown and off to the east, in a little house needing paint set down in a cinder yard. Ray saw it was the kind of neighborhood where folks pooled up who worked at all-night gas stations and convenience stores when they had jobs at all. Folks who left school at sixteen, walked off jobs, walked out on marriages, and nobody—teachers or kids, bosses or spouses—was sorry to see them go.

Dave sat on the fender of his car, picking the sleep out of the corners of his eyes. He had no fishing gear, only himself in a windbreaker advertising an out-of-business nightspot. It looked to Ray like he was shivering a little. When he made to climb in, Bonnie scooted forward to the edge of the seat. "This looks like a place where trolls live," she told him.

Dave smiled a little smile. "The gal my roommate's dating, she looks kind of like a troll. Maybe it is."

"Then we better get out of here." Bonnie cut her eyes at Ray.

All the way out the valley and on up Afton's Mountain, Bonnie held herself balanced with one hand against the dashboard, not wanting to touch any part of Dave and risk catching his cooties. Sherri could be that way too, blaming Ray when there was nothing to be blamed for, blaming him for what anybody could see were facts of the human condition. Dave was another person, different, but worth some consideration and respect. He woke up and lit up a smoke. "Shitty weather," he said.

"You shouldn't say that, it's cussing," Bonnie told him.

"What'd I say? 'Shit'? Shit's not cussing. Cussing's taking the Lord's name in vain. Shit. Shit's something you do, something everybody does."

"It's not nice." She looked at Ray and said, "Is it, Daddy?"

"Nice? What's not nice?" Dave was looking at Ray too.

"In our family, we don't say nasty words or swear words, honey."

Dave rolled his eyes up to the roof of the truck and blew out a plume of smoke. Then he said in a tired voice, "I know about you, man. I know about your kind of people. Nice people. Jesus don't know from nice."

"Jesus was nice," Bonnie said.

"You don't know what you're talking about, kid." And Dave rolled into a Technicolor movie of a Jesus seven stories high, trampling out the grapes of wrath like Godzilla in a bathrobe. Tall buildings would topple over; cars scatter off the highways like dried-up leaves. Every corner of the ocean would be swept clean of ships; whole pieces of the planet—football stadiums, parking lots, missile silos—would just be vaporized and replaced by big trees and little bushes full of berries. All the earth put back the way it was. "I bet you never thought of that, huh," Dave said, still talking in his soft, weary voice. "Heaven on earth, sure, but where would all this crap go?" He punched his cigarette at the windshield, but meant the highway they rode on, four-lane from sea to shining sea.

"Daddy," Bonnie said, and Ray could hear a panicked urgency in her voice.

"What do you expect me to do about it?" he asked Dave.

"Do about it? Why, you can take your foot off that accelerator and pull over and get out beside this truck and pray. Pray to Jesus. Down on your knees. She's big enough," Dave said, flipping his cigarette at Bonnie, "she's big enough too."

"Daddy," Bonnie said again, but Ray didn't answer. Instead he announced into the cab as if he'd just discovered it himself, "We used to come up here when I was a kid."

"That's nice," Dave said and took a drag on his cigarette, looked out the window, and fidgeted. Everybody was red in the face, maybe from the overheated cab.

"Daddy," Bonnie said again.

Ray had to pull off on top of Afton's Mountain just as they turned south on the Parkway so Bonnie could be sick. "Sorry," Dave said. He leaned against the bed of the truck while Ray sat on the grassy roadside holding Bonnie crying on his lap. It wasn't raining much at all now, but the fog had rolled over the road. Ray always marveled at how easily a child threw up, the vomit just seemed to slide right out her mouth and onto the grass. All her breakfast, the brown wads of cereal, the tiny bites of toast, the juice, was right there. He offered to take her into the little nearby restaurant and buy her another, but she shook her head no.

Down below them, under the fog and clouds, on the slick and rainy streets of Charlottesville, Sherri drove herself in the approximate direction of Dr. Roger's house. The dark heavy sky brought up the color, the yellow in the traffic lights and fireplugs, the greens and blues in the college students' slickers. Flashing between the beating wipers, color threatened to overwhelm her. Did she let herself know where she was headed when she put the key in the ignition? Sherri felt the presence of another car looming up behind her, urging her into a slower lane. She held her ground. He was an awful, awful man, yet he could serve some purpose in her life. She felt she was in danger, and she decided she wanted to be.

Nobody prayed on the Parkway roadside. Instead they climbed back in the truck where Ted lay sleeping in his baby seat. Ray thought about turning around. If Sherri hadn't been so pissy when they left, maybe he could have. They drove on. Crazy Dave had his vent window pushed all the way open so Bonnie wouldn't get sick anymore, while Ray ran the heater full blast to try to clear the window glass. All he could do was run the truck along the white line marking the shoulder and look for the turn to his lake. Ted was waking up and starting to squirm around in his car seat. Pretty soon he'd start hollering.

"We should go home, Daddy," Bonnie said severely.

"In a little while," Ray told her.

When Ray caught a glimpse from the road above, he wasn't sure it was a lake or a gouge in the green mountainside, a deep dark hole seen through the fog. "That's it." He could have heard it in his own voice; he didn't really want to go down there.

Ray's boat, which had looked sturdy and competent in his garage, was a puny thing threatened by every sharp stick and rough-edged rock down on the windy lakeshore. The hull wobbled with the small waves running under it. Maybe it would be more stable with four people, the cooler of sandwiches and pop, the rods and the can of worms holding it down. Dave said, "Hey, man, maybe I could take one of those rods and try fishing off the bank."

Standing on the side of this small lake, Bonnie was thinking even if her daddy was a smart man, he couldn't know everything. What did her daddy think a little boat could do? She was afraid for him; she saw him as somebody who needed taking care of. What could a princess do with a daddy like that? Bonnie started to cry.

"OK," Ray told her, "you can stay and fish with Dave or you can come in the boat with Ted and me." She looked over at Dave, who shrugged and smiled, then climbed into the boat. Ted hollered and flailed his arms around. "Look at that, Ted's ready to fish."

"Oh Daddy," Bonnie said.

Ray pulled the oars, and the boat moved out into the lake. Really, he thought, it rowed much better than you would think. The wind began to fall off, and as it did, the fog settled down on them. While Ray rowed, Crazy Dave, the pickup, the shoreline, and the mountain behind it all disappeared. All around them was whiteness and the sound of lapping water. Ted heard it and was soothed; he left off crying. Bonnie heard it and thought maybe this time her daddy would be all right. His funny boat would take them wherever he wanted to go.

And so Ray took up one of the old casting rods with a push-button reel and broke a fat worm in half and put it on the hook, cast it out for Bonnie and told her to watch her bobber. He did the same for himself. They sat in the foggy lake and waited.

No fish came for their worms.

Ray thought, how about it, fish? How about it, world? But the world had balled him into a big wad of cotton and gone off and left him. Where were his friends? Now was when he needed them, not to give him off-the-meter legal tips, or to put him onto some hot new bands. He needed them to sit in his boat with him in the fog and not get any bites either, to stick around until it was nearing nightfall, when they could all go home, take a hot shower, and eat dinner. Where were they now?

He looked at Ted and saw how his eyes took in the foggy color of the sky and returned it. "Having fun, buddy?" he asked him, but Ted didn't say anything. What if he never said anything? What if he turned out to be one of those big old guys you saw going around the shopping malls with a broom and a dustpan? A shaggy forty-year-old man trained up to the level of a good bird dog? Roll the window down and let him stick his head out on the way home and that would make him happy.

Fish had yet to come for their worms.

How long had it been? With his paint-speckled watch hanging on the gearshift in his truck, Ray had no choice but to sit in his boat in the fog, his boy asleep in his baby seat, his daughter gazing out at her bobber. Nothing but his bobber off to his left and Bonnie's off to his right, both of them still. Ray waited. He listened, and every now and then he thought he heard a plunk that could have been Dave casting from the bank. Ray wanted to call out, but he didn't.

Ray had been claustrophobic as a kid. Once his brothers and sisters had locked him in the coat closet under the stairs, and after a short while the pressing smells of mothballs and wool, the wooden limits he felt in all directions, caused him to holler out and go at the door so he had kicked out the bottom panel by the time his mother got there to let him out. There he had stood in the middle of the living room, his eyes still getting used to the light, still feeling the presence of a nearby power.

Now it was different. There weren't any walls holding him in, only fog. But the fog seemed like it might go on forever, the lake below them might be the kind he heard stories about when he was a kid, the kind where divers went down and down until they ran out of their air supply and came up without ever finding the bottom. How could he row his boat when one direction seemed as good as another?

Ray got scared. He got scared of everything. It wasn't just the things he wanted to happen, the things he always thought he could make happen, but everything that might and could happen whether he wished for it or not. It was as if the shores of this small lake were getting farther and farther away from him. Once again, he wanted to call out, but didn't. There was no point.

Then, as it often does in the mountains, the wind came up lightly and started rolling the fog away up the mountain. If Ray could have seen it from up above, it would have looked like a kid tearing the paper away from a present. Across the lake, the head of an old man in a roll-top hat popped out of the fog, then the rest of his body appeared in a cloudy mist shot through with golden sunlight. It looked as if he rode on a throne on top of the water. He turned his head toward Ray and his children and hollered out, "Howdy there. I thought I had this place all to myself."

When Ray and Bonnie hailed him back, he heard in their voices the forlorn cries of sailors set adrift. "What's the matter, not catching anything?" And he rowed toward them, working his oars one after the other like a bicyclist. He lifted out his stringer and showed them many shining fish, crappie, ring perch. "You got to fish down deep to get these," he told them as he took Ray's stringer and gave them half his catch.

"We were scared," Bonnie told him, "we were lonely."

"I expect so," the old man said. "Hardly a fit day. Now, you all go home and eat those fish." And he brought his boat about and rowed off into the lake.

Crazy Dave lay curled up asleep on the seat of the pickup, his rod thrown in the bed. When Ray opened the door, Bonnie said, "What's that funny smell?"

"Nothing to worry about," Ray told her. As they climbed in the truck, the mountain came out into the sunlight and stood there as it always had, stoop–shouldered and worn.

What, exactly, had happened after Sherri pulled into Dr. Roger's arcing driveway hidden by hedges? When Dr. Roger met her at the door, he had tried to act surprised. But beyond the marvels of cannonballs and tarnished swords, what else could such a guy have for Sherri? She wondered this herself, sitting alone with a drink in a grimy bar for college students. Her clothes, made foul and unfamiliar, did not seem to fit her right. She needed a bath, but that would mean going home and she wasn't ready for that. She wanted to give the rescue squad a chance to find the bodies, the police a chance to come to the house, for them to find nobody home so the guilt would fall fully on her shoulders.

When she was good and drunk, when the bar was full of college boys who grinned at her like they knew all about it, she made her way back to her car through the fresh, damp evening air. She drove home without seeing a sign of a policeman, and found her house pouring light from every window onto the rich green lawn.

Clean and bathed, Ted sat in his high chair, Bonnie at the table in her PJs. Ray was flipping a fish over in the skillet. Her family beamed at her. She saw Ted, she saw Bonnie. She saw that Ray remained the very Ray who had pulled out of the driveway that morning, and she thought she loved him still. And yet she felt the events of her own day hovering between them. Like a ghostly presence, what happened between her and Dr. Roger would hang around in the air of the house until she had the nerve to tell Ray what had happened. She wondered if she ever would.

"Somebody else caught those fish, Mom," Bonnie told her.

But Sherri already knew that, didn't she?

Key to the Kingdom

Rejoice not when thine enemy falleth,
and let not thine heart be glad when he stumbleth.
PROVERBS 24:17

There's a guy in every town who has a key to the gym, somebody who got ahold of it years ago and just forgot to give it back. It might be the high school math teacher who has always been good about chaperoning dances. Or the town cop who runs a peewee league on Saturdays. You'd want to be friends with such a guy so that the Sunday morning game everybody knows about but only a select few are actually invited to would be open to you.

In our town, that guy is T-Bird Chance. T-Bird Chance. It's the kind of name you only have to hear once to remember. And T-Bird likes to be remembered. He makes car loans at the bank. He says he's got the name for it when he hands out his card, shiny black with a thunderbird of Indian design outlined around his name. Don't ask him how he got his name, only women can ask him that and get a truthful answer. And don't ask how come he's got the key to the gym. That can be a touchy subject.

Inside the gym at nine in the morning on a spring day the sunlight slants across the blond wood floor, the air is cool and still, and the pleasing smell of years of accumulated sweat greets you at the door. T-Bird

Chance, the first one through, gives his old leather ball, worn brown as a walnut, five quick bounces and shoots. "Touch," he announces to his assembled pals as the ball takes three light hops on the rim before falling through. They smile. T-Bird is known for his touch.

This Sunday there are sixteen or seventeen, enough for three teams, which is the best. And by noon or so everybody has about as much as he wants. They look around for their wallets and keys and sweat clothes. T-Bird flips the ball into the back seat of his car, and they stand around shooting the shit. Except that it's such a beautiful day most of them end up wandering up the bank to the football field where the grass is still dewy and on across to the bleachers where T-Bird wrings out his T-shirt and spreads it to dry, takes his sweats and balls them into a pillow and stretches himself out in the sun.

Now you can see the design on his gym shorts, almost worn away from the washings, a basketball and the word *Maroons*. And if you know small college basketball you might think of the Roanoke College Maroons, a perennial, as the sports writers like to say, in Division III ball. Sure, you think, the way he runs the fast break, how easy he beats his man, drives through the double team. A little too fancy on the passes, a little too ready to take the shot himself, but then he has the key to the gym. How old is he, because in the light he shows his age, early thirties? None of his friends could say without thinking a minute. He played his high school ball right here, but that was some time back.

On this day, there is some talk of rabbit raising. Snell, who wears bib overalls for his sweat clothes and doesn't own a jockstrap, has sent off to the state agricultural department for literature. "Rabbits will," he pronounces, "fuck you to riches." It's a pleasing idea, one that might put these pals in the mind of going on home if they are lucky enough to have some permanent understanding: a wife who still loves the name of Jesus, home from church by now but still in her stockings and heels. Or an easier kind of gal still drowsing in bed in an old flannel shirt.

"Boys," says T-Bird, "we got this four-by-four Ford Ranger down on the parking lot. It's a real cherry. Claim it by the first of the month and all you got to do is take over payments." He talks lying flat on the swaybacked bleacher with the sleeve of his sweatshirt pulled up over his eyes, his voice oddly hollow. He sounds like he could be in a trance.

Nobody says a thing. That's Bernard Thomas's truck and they all know how he lost it back to the bank. "How 'bout it, Claw, ain't that just what you been looking for?"

Claw is Mike Barber, called Claw by T-Bird and nobody else because he has bad hands, can't handle the ball, and the Ranger is in fact just what he's been looking for. "Haven't got the coin, partner," Mike tells him.

All of them have heard the talk that T-Bird has been fucking Mag Hickey. Mag is Bernard Thomas's wife. T-Bird has fucked plenty of women, though. In fact that's one of the little bonuses of the Sunday game, to hear about T-Bird's Saturday night. How many times have they witnessed him roll up to the side door of the gym, the only one the key fits, still duded up in his party clothes, and have to change in the corner while everybody else is warming up? "Put it to you," he gloats after beating his man for a layup, "Did it to her last night, you this morning."

Thinking about Mag Hickey makes everybody feel shitty and cold, which is not how they want to feel after three hours of busting ass full court. Knowing when to quit is the trick, before everybody is strung up and down the floor and missing the layups so it's getting to be a raggedy game.

T-Bird shivers, feeling like a cloud has covered up the sun, but if he took that shirt sleeve off his face he'd see no clouds up above him. "Speak up, guys, this is a real buy."

Mag Hickey is the baby of the locally famous Hickey family. You'll still hear people talk about Buckeye Hickey, who because of some mysterious childhood ailment, some say it was a touch of polio, could never hold his head up straight. But he knocked the bottom out of the basket every night he played. There are those who say he taught T-Bird Chance everything he knows about basketball. Now he drives a pop truck five days a week, preaches up at the Holiness Church, and is well thought of around town though he never married, for the obvious reason.

T-Bird, though, was married once. It lasted two or three years. His ex- still thinks the Sunday game was what broke them up, that he cared more about playing basketball with his pals than he did about her. But there have been many Sunday mornings when you could have driven up around the school building and treated yourself to the spectacle of a dozen or so grown men huddled under the eight-by-six portico, stood up by their collective date.

Now nobody says a thing. Snell, considering Mag and the truck, thinks, fuck yourself to riches, but wouldn't ever say it aloud. The bleachers creak from their stiff movements as they gather their scattered stuff. It's best to clear out while they can still have their contented sighs and stretches. This is what the Sunday game is for. They better watch out before it gets away from them.

Down by the cars T-Bird says, "Mike," and Claw is so surprised to hear T-Bird call his given name that he turns around beaming. "Take a look at this." And T-Bird reaches him one of his shiny black cards from out of the console between the real leather seats of his car. A figure is scribbled across its back. "That's all it takes," says T-Bird.

As T-Bird drives off, Snell, who grows marijuana plants out on his place, takes the card out of Mike Barber's hand. "Buy it and I'll have your ass," he says.

I wish I could take you on a helicopter ride over our town so you could see the school, built in the fifties about a mile west of town and situated on the road up the valley where nobody much used to live. It was pastureland, and now more and more people live there in double wide trailers and Jim Walter homes. You could follow T-Bird's progress as he drives up this road with a lot on his mind and nothing to do, up the head of the valley and over the hill to Horsepen, then Bishop, and back into Tazewell and Bluefield and home again to the Dairy Bar for a chocolate shake because you'll find almost all the roads around here loop around to home if you follow them long enough. T-Bird has driven them all many times and has found his pleasure in the familiarity of each twisty curve, glad to know he'll turn up back where he started from.

When he went to Roanoke College that's about what happened. You couldn't say college wasn't what he expected because he wasn't expecting anything at all. He remembers it as a place where people went around talking crazy talk. He thought he knew about going to school, but this was different, people talking, talking in his classes, talking in the dormitories, in the cafeteria, even in the small campus post office where T-Bird got so he hated to go, never a goddamn thing for him there. All that talk, and basketball didn't work out for him either. Nobody told him he wasn't going to be the star.

Now there's nothing for him to do. He'll wash his car and go in and watch part of a baseball game on TV. Around six he'll take a chance and call Mag Hickey at home. He's been told that Bernard Thomas sometimes goes to see his mother on Sunday afternoons. That's all he does now, go to church and to see his mother, driving himself ten miles an hour like a farmer.

This same morning Buckeye Hickey preaches that you can't be tempted by the devil unto paths you didn't already want to follow. His sister Maggie, sitting right there where she belongs with Bernard, is taking his words in. She is always sure Preacher Buckeye's sermons are for her alone.

What can she do? She has read the same thing in Ann Landers, that you can't be led into temptation unless you want to go. And she has wanted to write Ann and say this isn't so, you can go down against your will, just as a drowning man doesn't want to drown but goes under just the same. She felt it happen that way in T-Bird's car, him kissing her on the lips and face and then her neck and then opening the winged collar of her blouse and kissing her in there. He would have kissed her on her breasts but she grabbed his hand and stopped him as he was trying to undo her third button, grabbed him so hard the button popped.

She was too nervous to thread the needle to sew it back, T-bird had to thread it for her. And while she sat there in her bra sewing, all she could think about was that it was her good bra, the one with the little lace inserts, the one she only wore on Sundays in the presence of Jesus and Bernard afterward. She had put it on that morning on purpose, then, because Buckeye says if you are attentive to the will of the Lord there can be no accidents, everything is to an end, a good end or bad end. Sitting there putting that button on under the map light, Mag was already pushed closer to T-Bird than if she had let him go on.

When T-Bird calls, Bernard is in the kitchen fixing himself a stack of peanut butter crackers. Even before Mag picks up the phone she knows. She counts to five while muffling T-Bird's voice with her hand, then she says, "We don't want any," and hangs up.

It shouldn't have mattered if people had seen her riding in T-Bird's low black car. They had, of course, and were talking it around. But if she hadn't had to sit there half naked in the quiet of the car while he watched her sew the button on, people could have said whatever they wanted.

Just after the Sunday game Snell rides Mike Barber up to his place to show off his rabbits fresh from the Farmers' Market. Snell's built himself some chicken-wire hutches on the shady side of the old barn — one for Rocky, a doughy white buck, one for Angelique, his slimmer mate. "They aren't going to make you rich in separate cages," Mike tells him, but Snell says he hasn't gotten that far yet. He even has to admit he's not sure these are especially good breeding stock. All he knows is what the old bastard who sold them said, that you could sell the meat to an outfit in Knoxville that made rabbit TV dinners to sell in Europe since Americans think bunnies are too cute to eat. There's another outfit in New York that buys the skins to trim moccasins and line gloves and such.

"Who's going to kill them?" Mike asks while Snell's two grubby kids push a variety of weeds through the mesh to test the rabbits' eating habits.

"Me. Haven't you ever shot a rabbit and dressed it?"

Mike says he hasn't, that he's never shot anything. Snell hasn't either, but he still thinks Mike is too soft, too ready to say he's sorry for every bad pass, every rebound that gets away. Mike is only in the Sunday game because he's the assistant principal's son-in-law. "You got to be a hard-ass if you want anything in this world," Snell tells him, "look at T-Bird."

They look at the rabbits, so white and stupid, nosing at the bunches of dandelions on the floor of their cages, and consider T-Bird Chance, his slick suits and his German car. You might be somebody who knows how little bank tellers make and be surprised that T-Bird can afford such a car since that's all he really is, a chief teller of what used to be a real bank but now has been bought out and bought out again by bigger concerns. Down in Richmond they don't think they need an executive officer in an operation the size of our town's, so they put T-Bird back in the office where you could go in and talk to him about a car loan. But during that period when he's supposed to be sifting out the facts of your financial situation, he's on the phone to Bluefield. They make all the decisions up there.

All people in town know is that he's the one who made the call to Bernard Thomas asking him to turn his truck in, a little courtesy before the letter came by registered mail. It seems like back in the early summer Bernard Thomas went crazy or something. It's reached the point where he can't go to work anymore even though nothing is wrong with him. He gets up in the morning and just sits on the edge of the bed and somehow isn't able to bring himself to get dressed. At first he was just slow. Sitting there with one sock on and the other in his hand, Bernard would be staring at that sock like maybe it would speak and tell him the secrets of God's big world, or maybe say something simpler, like to get off his ass and get moving. Finally, he could no longer go out in the county and sell life insurance, which is a shame, he was so good at it.

Maybe Mag Hickey stopped loving him and maybe he knew it. Maybe he came in one afternoon and she was standing in the doorway between the kitchen and dining room looking right through him the way we all had at one time or another. He took pictures for a hobby and was pretty good, people asked him to do their wedding pictures and class reunions. Maybe that's why it was hard to remember afterwards whether he'd been there or not.

Old man Ellis Hickey is still alive. He hasn't been out of his house for years, just sits in the kitchen with a cup of coffee. They say he keeps a beard now down to his waist and in his frailness he's like nothing more than a puff of smoke hanging in the air. He and Buckeye keep house together. "What," Ellis wonders, "will we do for Sister?" Maggie hasn't been coming around. He knows what it means.

What Mag told Buckeye was that she got tired of having to be the one to make the coffee and fill up the thermos and start cooking his eggs before calling Bernard again to get up. She started leaving him at the table in his pajamas, then in the bed. She had to get to work on time herself, didn't she?

Snell doesn't know a damned thing really, but it doesn't matter, he's been looking for a way to get T-Bird Chance for some time. T-Bird shoots too much and he's never said thanks for an outlet pass his whole basketball life. Snell tells Mike Barber somebody more reliable ought to keep the key to the gym.

Sitting there with the whole of his face hot from Mag Hickey's voice on the phone line, looking at the TV and for a minute not knowing what was going on, though it was "The Wonderful World of Disney," the castle and fireworks he's seen a thousand times, T-Bird knows he's getting in trouble.

Several of the loans down at the bank have gone sour, and Bernard's wasn't even one he'd been counting. It's not his fault, but he senses in a vague way, the way he can feel somebody coming from the blind side to double team him, that up in Bluefield the sleepy looking guy in the baggy suit might be looking for somebody to rub the blame on. After all, what else is T-Bird there for? And there's this teller, a girl really, just out of high school, T-Bird picked her for her legs. When he knocked her up, he paid for the abortion, but now that he's seeing Mag Hickey that little girl has a dark look in her eye. And there is Mag. When he first took her in his arms, she trembled.

T-Bird says, "You better get your act together, son," starts hustling around gathering up his socks and sweats and a week's worth of dirty underwear to take to his mother to wash. That first time when she slid out of his car, she didn't let herself look back. T-Bird feels a tightening sensation in his throat. He's felt it once or twice before, he knows what it means.

Why? She always wears that shade of stockings that make her legs look orange. Mag Hickey, skinny with a freckled face and dark brown hair she wears waved like some woman twice her age, is nobody's idea of pretty.

That little teller, though, had sucked his cock, grinned at him square in the face with her bright green eyes before she took him in her mouth. T-Bird had sat up in his bed that night thinking about her look and trying to decide why he didn't like it.

———————

Buckeye Hickey only went to see T-Bird play once. He could see his own small basketball tricks in T-Bird's game, but covered over now with a mess of dips and fakes that had nothing to do with fooling the defense. His picture was in the Bluefield paper once a week then, and it wasn't the team but T-Bird that got the headlines. You couldn't blame him for that, but you could fault him for the look of stricken amazement he put on whenever he was called for a foul, holding a pinch of his jersey out to check his number like it must be some kind of mistake. His first look after a layup was not to find his man but toward the stands. For Buckeye Hickey, who had done everything he could to get people to forget he was there at all, who remembered when he was a sophomore how they laughed even in his own gym at his head set crooked on his neck, it was too much to take. He left at the end of the third quarter with our team way ahead and the coach still letting T-Bird play.

When Bernard Thomas finally leaves home, he finds himself going up the Valley to Buckeye's house instead of to his mother's like he told Mag. Even on Sunday he's afraid. He's afraid of coal trucks that take turns too wide, of every car idling at a stop sign waiting to lunge out from the intersection in front of him, of kids on their bicycles, of dogs running loose. He's afraid of falling rocks. Once on the road to Grundy, Bernard saw a rotten chunk of sandstone smashed into the roof of a brand-new Chevrolet. He tells Buckeye that at any moment things can spin out of control. He hears crashing sounds in his ears, braces himself for sudden impact. He tells Buckeye all the pain he knows.

Buckeye Hickey is always filled with wonder at the Holy Spirit, how it can pass through tinted glass and enter into the interior of a Japanese car and dwell among the chrome knobs and black dials, the sticky vinyl upholstery. He prays out loud with one hand pinching the bridge of his nose, just as he does in his church, and Bernard silently prays with him right there in the dirt driveway facing the basket where Buckeye once practiced his craft.

T-Bird calls back and asks Mag Hickey to go riding with him after work, to let him pick her up. He says he has things to tell her. She sits on the couch holding the phone just near enough to hear and doesn't answer him, but when T-Bird hangs up, he knows she will be waiting.

What T-Bird cannot know is how fast he's coming up on one of those blind intersections we have so many of here in the mountains. Loving speed was always one of his faults, and somehow he never remembers that moment just after it's too late and events start stacking up around him. Bernard Thomas could have warned him.

So when Buckeye Hickey comes in the bank, T-Bird feels the color coming up in his face and has to remind himself he's got nothing to be ashamed of. It's Wednesday and Buckeye always does his banking on Wednesdays, the day his route swings him through town, to the two little groceries and the two beer joints where Buckeye will shoot a game of pool as long as there's no money involved. Buckeye Hickey is also known for his touch.

When he asks one of the girls for T-Bird, nobody imagines he's come for a loan. This old bank has walnut paneling about five feet up. Little brass rails run along the counter separating customers and help, a re-minder of when banking could be a rougher business. There are no doors to the offices, just little gates. Inside the old vice-president's office, T-Bird is sitting, listening to Buckeye being let back behind the windows, listening to the chitchat die to an idle while all three tellers cock their ears to his stall in the corner.

Buckeye sits down in the straight chair without arms, a chair set about four feet away, an uncomfortable distance from T-Bird's dark wide desk. T-Bird hangs a foot on an open bottom drawer and smiles out at Buckeye, who, stripped of his cheap Sunday suit and his Bible, looks like any other busted hillbilly, red wrists dangling out of the sleeves of his Double Cola windbreaker. "Not much of a team this year, was it?" T-Bird says. He prides himself on having a specially tailored line of bullshit to suit every customer.

People who watched Buckeye Hickey play remember he made slowness an art, running with a sloppy splay-footed gait, walking when he could get away with it. Nobody on the other team took much notice until he had snuck across the lane and was standing there with his big hand stuck out for the ball, the guy who was supposed to be guarding him caught up on Buckeye's skinny butt. Once a man got hung on his butt, there wasn't anything to do except to watch as Buckeye caught the ball and threw a lazy hook against the backboard all in one motion.

Buckeye didn't get to see a single game last season. He looks at T-Bird with his preacher look, like he's somehow x-raying the soul and is pained by what he sees there. T-Bird hasn't had much experience with guilt, but he's still able to fight off most of it. What the hell, he didn't drive Bernard Thomas crazy. Buckeye says, "I was wondering about Bernard's truck."

T-Bird's knocked off balance for a minute. His shoe slips off its rest and he asks, "You want to buy it?" You could say Buckeye Hickey has T-Bird on his butt just now since T-Bird knows even as he says it that Buckeye hasn't stopped in to talk about buying a truck.

For Buckeye, it's not as simple a move as you might think. Because even though Bernard hadn't spoken of T-Bird and his wife taken in adultery, others had, in that cruel but necessary way of sly comments and jokes, until even a preacher glimpsing the fluttering tail of such talk could get the idea. Except that Buckeye is thinking that to name the act and accuse T-Bird of it would also require that he as a Christian be prepared to forgive him. And he is not.

So Buckeye limits his talk to his brother-in-law's frame of mind, which he considers to be "one of those things," losing his confidence is all it amounts to. He will be back to work in no time. All he needs is some room to breathe. All he needs is for people to get off his back, for people to stay out of his business and mind their own. "It's a damned nosy town," Reverend Hickey says with desperate conviction.

Huddled briefly in the bosom of God, Bernard had been comforted. But Buckeye Hickey knows that except for those like his father who are strong enough to look God in the face all the time, there's only a little rest stop there. If Bernard can find no love in men, he won't find much in Jesus either.

As Buckeye leaves the bank building in shame, even the girls at the tellers' windows know how bad he's been beaten. They have only themselves to blame for thinking the simple deception involved in making a soft hook shot look easy could have anything at all to do with the way people will do one another. T-Bird follows him to the door and watches as he goes back to his pop truck, his work pants flapping way above his ankle bones.

Buckeye's words don't do anything to change T-Bird's mind; he can't even convince himself. Maybe if he had only known that T-Bird was nothing but a flunky, it would have changed things. Maybe if he could have seen into T-Bird's desk full of nothing but old ballpoint pens and key rings left over from the former management, he could have said what he needed to say. Maybe so.

But even then it was too late. On Monday, Mag Hickey had sat outside the place she worked, that mining supply place in the prefab building on Brushfork Road, waiting in her car for T-Bird to come take her riding. His speed through the corners, shifting down so the car felt pushed into the roadbed, that slight sense of vertigo was getting to her. They pulled off at one of those little muddy roads out by Falls Mills Dam, a place each had known since high school. When his hands crawled up her legs, she felt his touch was electric. She wanted to say, "not in the car." She wanted to lay in a bed with T-Bird, where even naked and even with somebody she couldn't really say she knew, she would feel released from worrying about Bernard. There wasn't time for any of that.

———

Sometimes, T-Bird knows, a player will feel like he's lost his touch. The ball gets heavy and slick, a dull weight he pushes up to the basket.

He can't even follow his own shot. It happens to everybody, but when it happens to T-Bird his pals know to give him plenty of room. On those days, there's liable to be a fight as he blames the guy who's guarding him, making up fouls that never really happened, or forces his way into impossible positions to shoot from and then shoots anyway. "Fuck it," he says, "and fuck you too," when another one rims out.

That's exactly what he's saying a few Sundays later when the assistant principal walks through the gym and goes on back into the locker rooms and the coaches' office. What's he doing here? a few guys might think, then dismiss it. It's his building, you know. But when the ball rolls dead and everybody stacks up at the water fountains, here he comes in those giant crepe-soled shoes he wears, squeaking onto the floor and squinting around. "Who's in charge here, Mike?" he says to his son-in-law, and the guys form a semicircle around him. They all remember being just a little in trouble with him back in their high school pasts, so the tone of his voice brings a different uncomfortable thought back to each. Except why would Snell, who was in trouble all the time, be the first to pipe up? "Chance," Snell says, "Chance has the key." And the assistant principal won't even believe him until Mike, red-faced, nods.

It's over that fast. The assistant principal says other groups have been asking to use the gym too, and if one group is to be let in, then they all will, "and you fellows know we can't have that." Poor old Claw. He's so ashamed of his part in it that most of the guys think he's innocent.

What was it that T-Bird had to talk to Mag Hickey about? She wonders herself. They never do anything except get in his car and drive. If it's dark maybe they sneak into his apartment, if not they go back to the trusty muddy roads. Sneaking and lying kept her busy enough for a while, anything that wasn't Bernard was good enough for a while. Now she wonders. She's heard all the stories about T-Bird Chance. It's only a matter of time until the green-eyed girl at the bank will have her turn to smirk, God knows she's not smirking now.

T-Bird does talk if Mag would only listen. As they drive he tells her about the Sunday game. It's not what you imagine, all his glory, but everything, who's played well or poorly, what small basketball miracles he's witnessed, because whenever a bunch of guys get together to play a little ball, wonderful moments will unfold, as good as any you're liable to see on TV, allowing for scale and proportion. T-Bird is telling her everything he loves.

But of course just now nobody has a key to the gym.

Oh hell. That damned Snell really is making some money on the rabbit ranch. Drive past his place and look at how those cages have been multiplying. Snell loves to show people around, coming out of the barn in his rubber apron covered in blood, "You just missed the ritual sacrifice." And picking up a rabbit by its scruff, he says, "First you fuck, then you die." The rabbit looks around, panicked.

In a penny-ante way, Snell suffers too. There is no Sunday game. At first they try the goals out behind the elementary school where the school maintenance people did such a shitty job leveling the asphalt. Then a carload goes over to Bramwell to try to get in their game. But they have their own bunch, and besides, nobody really wants to play with Bramwell. You can rent the Y in Bluefield. You can wait till afternoon and play behind the Baptist church.

T-Bird could think of something. Except he hasn't been around. Lately T-Bird has been too busy for the Sunday game. Mag Hickey has quit going to church. Sitting in T-Bird's kitchen with their coffee and the paper, they have gotten to be as up-front about adultery as you can get in a little town like ours.

Mag Hickey doesn't bother to make up lies for Bernard. She decides he'll believe anything. Sitting up waiting for her to slip in the door near dawn, he watches old movies where drunks and weaklings are filled with resolve through just a nudge to their integrity. For Bernard, though, nothing happens. He should be like Jimmy Stewart and with the help of improved posture confront his wife and T-Bird Chance. If he can't shame them into doing right by just showing up wherever they are, he might have to beat the mortal shit out of T-Bird. Bernard knows he can't do either. He concludes he must be getting what he deserves.

The week T-Bird and Mag sneak off to Myrtle Beach, what passes for God's wrath comes down on our town. Reverend Hickey preaches a sermon full of torment and rage. Those who are there say Bernard seems to find some comfort in the notion of the blind leading the blind into a ditch. Four souls are brought to Christ, an unexpected bonus, I'd guess, but Preacher Hickey takes no satisfaction in whatever sins he's shook out of his congregation.

Knowing T-Bird is out of the bank, the bigwig in the baggy suit drives over to our town, and there's a brief rumor that we'll have a vice-president again. The girls don't know how to take it. They've gone sour on T-Bird, but the way this guy stares at them makes their skin creep. He leaves word for Bernard Thomas's Ford Ranger to be driven up to Bluefield and leaves a sealed letter for T-Bird. He can put up those shiny cards, he's not chief teller at our bank anymore.

Down on the beach surrounded by hundreds of people, T-Bird and Maggie imagine they're the only unhappy ones there. The ocean is cold and the sand is full of litter, so they go back to their room that stinks of a million cigarettes. T-Bird hates the smell of smoke. They fuck hard and talk dirty and barely manage to come. Afterwards, the TV broken, they decide there's not a decent radio station in town.

Bernard takes the garden hose and runs it from the tailpipe into the window of Maggie's car. He reclines the seat and that's where the paper boy finds him, curled up on his side like maybe he's just sleeping. Reverend Hickey weeps at the thought of how little the Holy Spirit can sometimes do, how sometimes it enters in despite the noise and pain and how other times it bounces right off like a beam of sunlight on the windshield. The state troopers find T-Bird and Maggie to give them the news. It seems like everybody in town knew where they'd run off to.

Now it's gotten to be fall. Mike Barber got a key to the gym from his father-in-law after football season started. Those other groups that might be wanting to use the gym never came up. Now it's a different crowd. Mike and his short, slow friends take forever to play a game to twenty-one. At breaks, they talk about starting a chapter of the Jaycees, about making things happen in this town. Maybe you could get something to do with computers started here, you can do computers just about anywhere nowadays. Ask Snell to play, he'll say he'd rather tend his rabbits. Ask him if he's rich yet.

Outside, it's raining like hell. The football field still shows the signs of Friday night's game. Some archeologist coming on the scene would wonder: the thousands of pocks left in the yellow clay, the wadded gobs of tape, abandoned chin-strap buckles, forearm pads, dirty foam cups blown out into the field and squashed. The site of some cataclysmic event where people cleared out in a hurry, but why?

Mag Hickey goes back to church on a day when Reverend Buckeye takes his message from Proverbs. It's been a long time. She missed Bernard's funeral. Her hair is cut short and brushed to the side. She wears a black dress and black stockings and shoes. People are surprised at how good she looks. It doesn't matter, she's traveled well beyond vanity. She tells Buckeye she guesses it's her turn to suffer and he doesn't disagree.

When she finally remarries it will be to a short doughy man. She won't talk to T-Bird, she even has her number changed, won't read the letters he keeps sending her for years. Which is too bad, because he will finally find his voice and speak his love to her. Despite all the shit he'll pull, all the shit you'll no doubt hear about, T-Bird Chance will always love Mag Hickey.

T-Bird Chance pulls his car to the side door of the gym. He can see the warm yellow light glowing out the high windows. He bangs on the doors with his fists, but nobody can hear him over the rumble of running feet and the bouncing ball. It's a bright pumpkin-orange ball, one of the team's balls since Mike's key fits all the doors, even the one to the equipment room. T-Bird goes back around to the locker room door and bangs there too just in case somebody might be in the can and hear him. Nobody does of course. It's raining and the game is tied at fifteen. The thought of T-Bird Chance never enters their minds.

What about that T-Bird? The one T-Bird Chance got his name from? It's sitting up in Dewey Schrader's junkyard full of so much Bondo it might float, done up in a ninety-nine-dollar powder-blue paint job. It was a piece of shit the day he bought it. Anybody could have told him.

Unified Field Theory

Things happen, ask Hawkins. Up above, a jet labors in the thick dirty air. What's to keep it from falling, its skinny wings? Nothing is holding it up there but slippery molecules of air; any minute now it could drop like a rock, couldn't it? Hawkins thinks we all hold that plane up there by an act of collective concentration. Each and every one of us looks into the sky as we drive along in our cars, go to the bank, mow the grass; and, with our looks, little by little, we help that airplane make its way.

Hawkins jogs religiously along the roads around his apartment complex. He watches the planes inbound for Douglas Airport, so slow and low he can read the writing on their sides, see the small faces at the windows. Landings are the trickiest part. If nobody showed up at the airport to meet that planeload of loved ones and helped will it safely to a three-point landing, it could never happen. In the old days, it took a whole field full of Frenchmen to help Lindbergh cross the Atlantic. Now everybody has more confidence, so maybe it's easier. It's deceptive.

Bjorn Toulouse is temporarily stranded as a waitress in a truck stop off I-85 where drivers in their tractor caps read her name tag and don't get it. Next week, she decides, she will call herself Peggy Sue. Hawkins pines for her every morning when, turning into the driveway of their complex, he sees her just off the night shift sitting on her concrete stoop, her teapot and newspaper to comfort her. She has a hole in the toe of her black tights—Hawkins would kiss that pink toe if she'd let him.

Hawkins looks fit as a horse, but in ten years he'll be reduced to walking with a limp; his knees will betray him. Pain is everywhere waiting to ambush us. Now that his parents are divorced, he is never far from his mother's constant misery. His father didn't know love when it kicked him in the ass. He's lying in the hospital where he stands a good chance of going out of this life as stupid as when he came in. Hawkins feels frozen by rage and terror. So he watches the plane and wishes he could be more helpful, but he has little hope.

Hawkins thinks he saved Bjorn Toulouse's life once. Out in the universe, whole worlds have collisions. Every day. Mostly, we don't even notice. But sometimes a chance intersection changes everything. That's what happened when Hawkins went through the door at the T-Bar Truck Stop. A particularly ornery trucker was trying to put the make on Bjorn Toulouse and she was telling him a story about her big and nasty boyfriend who would adjust his face when Hawkins and two other guys from his warehouse walked in. "Here he comes now," she said.

Every day on his jog, Hawkins passes the same man and wife walking. The man wears a bright blue and green windbreaker and grins fiercely, a grin Hawkins recognizes from his own boyhood face when he fought to master the bicycle without training wheels. It was a long fight; gravity is cruel. Always, there was his father somewhere behind him, giving him an unexpected little push off, hollering out some false words of encouragement. He couldn't hide his anger when Hawkins lost his balance yet again. It should have come easier.

Bjorn Toulouse gave Hawkins and his pals free coffee and doughnuts. Since she believed in luck, nothing surprised her. She recognized Hawkins from his jogging and judged him another exercise addict. Now she saw he was a lonesome guy too, on his way to buying a thousand cups of coffee trying to work this angle he suddenly had on her life. Here's luck, then. She let him drive her home and taught him how to cast the I-Ching using six pennies, thinking that would keep him busy for a while.

That man walking is a surprisingly young man. You'd see it if you were just to concentrate on his face and use your imagination to relax it. He throws one leg loosely ahead and pulls his weight over it; the back leg comes reluctantly along, toes dragging. His wife has both arms wrapped around him like he was steady as a tree, the way a young girl will hold onto the first boy she ever loves. Maybe this man was that boy. Maybe they own one of the big rambling houses out on Roger's Quay Road, maybe they have a second house on Hilton Head Island. Twenty years ago, they never could have imagined themselves coming to this space in time, but here they are. She talks him through every step he takes.

You might think the strongest bonds in the universe are atomic bonds. It takes a mushroom cloud to break an atom to bits, but Hawkins knows the bonds of love are stronger.

The doctors have put Hawkins' father where the patients wander up and down the halls lonely as clouds. The psychiatric wing. It's crazy to call him depressed when his heart is the problem. It's lost its sense of purpose and even the small pacemaker he wears in a pocket stitched into his skin can't seem to fix it. The last time Hawkins tried to see him, the old man told him to get the hell out, mad that he couldn't take the whole world in his own hands and shape it.

To what extent, Hawkins wonders, you might wonder too, is he part of the problem? His apartment is neater than you'd expect. Along his bedroom wall he keeps the boxes for his clothes, in the living room, his shopping bags of important papers: a bag for bills and receipts, one for newspaper clippings, another for letters from friends. He finds the newspapers stingy with the truth, but has learned to watch and assemble the small clues they offer.

Hawkins owns a Ford the color of tomato soup. Lately it seems to him that it's beginning to take on the consistency of soup too; the surface is beginning to break up. Things fall apart. What was once a whole car or a house or even a mountain is now just a pile of rust or dust, just nothing. Molecules are, it turns out, mostly nothing. When you account for all the neutrons and electrons and other bits and pieces, there's a lot of room unaccounted for, full of nothing.

He's read that out in a cave in New Mexico somebody has stored barrels of water. If you were to go down there, that's what you'd see, barrels and barrels of water. It's not even heavy water like in a war movie about Nazis and the bomb. But special instruments are testing it, waiting to prove that little by little that water is changing, changing into nothing at all. Hawkins clipped the article and tossed it into his shopping bag.

His mother, he thinks, seems smaller all the time. She spent much of her life worrying about her hair. There just wasn't enough of it, and no amount of perming or coloring or body building treatments did any good. Now she wears it short and plain. Hawkins thinks she may yet reach beauty through her pain.

Hawkins likes to think of molecules as marbles. A large blue marble would be oxygen, a small clear marble would be hydrogen. Zinc would be gray, neon purple. Sometimes you bump them together and they stick. Sometimes nothing happens, or maybe they fly apart. Love is like that.

Bjorn Toulouse told Hawkins once her favorite color was black—it holds in the heat, she said. "Paint your car black," she told him, "but not like that," pointing across the way to a Camaro so shiny it wiggled in the sun. You want to hold heat in, everything in, she thought. Pieces are always breaking off as you move through the world. Just a walking pace is enough to sheer off bits of skin; don't run, don't ride with the window open, try not to stand under fans or in front of air conditioners.

Think of the Cloud Chamber. Think of a guy shooting electrons at tinfoil, just like the county fair. And just like the county fair, you can shoot and shoot and not hit a damned thing. Then, like maybe a cartoon or a comedy show, a guy will turn his back and fire his last shot over his shoulder and knock over the duck. There it goes, a shattered bit of atom making its clumsy way across the Cloud Chamber. Scientists who do this kind of work claim the patterns are beautiful. It's something most of us will never see.

Does that explain what's holding Hawkins back? He should just walk over to her stoop. "Forget the doubts and fears creeping in your heart" was what his fortune from the Chinese take-out told him the other night. The I-Ching, with all its charts and tables, was too hard. Except for taping the strip of paper to his refrigerator, he hasn't acted.

"How's your father?" Bjorn Toulouse hollers across to him.

Throughout his life, Hawkins' father has been his enemy, yet Hawkins loves him. He learned in his kidhood there was no point crying over a skinned knee when all his father told him was to be a Marine. How much would Hawkins suffer to prove that he loved him? In those school days, he knew no limits. Standing over a halfback with the breath knocked out of him, Hawkins roared like King Kong. Surely his father had loved him then.

What's there to say? Every day an eagle comes and eats the old man's heart out. Then, thanks to the miracle of modern medicine, it grows back again at night and the whole thing starts over. Who's to say he doesn't deserve it? Hawkins tells Bjorn. "You wouldn't want to see him."

Now, older and in no significant ways wiser, Hawkins has passed the point where there are no halfbacks left to tackle. He could beat the shit out of his old man, frail and puny now, and in their bassackwards way of loving this might pass for proof.

"Call me Al," the old man told Hawkins' college pals. He flashed his credit cards and bought them pizza and beer. They loved him for it. It should have been easy to be his kid; all Hawkins had to do was show some respect and do anything that might show to Al's credit. Somehow, Hawkins could never manage to do enough.

"Aw, man, are we talking tubes and shit?" Bjorn asks him. "Because if that's what it is, I say you take him out of there and get him into a holistic healing place." She pours her green tea into a china cup.

"It's the loony bin." On his father's floor at the hospital, Hawkins noticed that there was none of that rubbing alcohol clinical smell. Instead it's like there are dirty diapers hidden around somewhere. Maybe some of them did it in their pants. "He's depressed."

"You know the part in *Duck Soup* when Harpo knocks against the radio and 'Stars and Stripes Forever' comes on? That's when I gave up on depression. I decided I would never try to kill myself again."

Bjorn Toulouse is embarrassed to remember those days—she tried to eat diet pills, that's all she had, as a dramatization of how bad she wanted out of her life with this jerk bicycle mechanic. After watching the movie, she felt so good she forgot about being miserable for three weeks, then wrote him a note, taped it on the bathroom mirror, crammed her stuff in a laundry bag, and left. A month later he found out where she was living, called her up, and said he had herpes.

"You could come to the hospital with me," Hawkins says to her.

A hospital is like a gale-force wind. Bjorn Toulouse can't go there, just like she can't go to funerals or weddings. "I'll cook you breakfast instead." If he says "please," she decides, she will have to go with him, this is the inevitable payback for using him to scrape that creepy trucker off her leg. But he doesn't have to say a thing. When she sees his forehead puckered with need, she gives in.

"Why's he crazy anyway?"

"He's decided he's dying."

"So what's new?" says Bjorn Toulouse.

There are too many cars in the world, everybody knows that. It's not them, but their rushing around him, always exceeding the speed limit, that scares Hawkins. Things happen. As if he's watching a bad movie, Hawkins thinks in jumps from his view behind the wheel to another angle, a view some demon with a hand-held camera can get: a wheel with its lug nuts sheering wobbles, ready to break loose and find its own path. Master cylinders secretly drip their fluids away. Accelerator cables look for a way of sticking. Hawkins' brain switches from an image of him and Bjorn Toulouse happily motoring along to one of a wobbling wheel.

"You want me to drive?" says Bjorn. "You better quit that coffee."

Hawkins says, "See this intersection? A couple of years ago, a guy got wasted here. Another guy pulled up beside him at the light and shot him."

Bjorn Toulouse crosses herself and looks back at the place, a Krispy Kreme doughnut shop sits on the corner. "No wonder."

"They didn't even know each other."

"Kismet," she says.

"Listen, no religion, OK?" he asks her.

"Oh God, you don't have him at the Catholic place, do you? I can't face any nuns, they give me flashbacks." Bjorn Toulouse was raised Catholic and went to Catholic school where she lost her faith when they cut the hem out of her skirt at the flag-raising ceremony. Now she believes in macrobiotics. She doesn't understand how they work, but is confident they'll give you long life. What do you get out of a religion these days anyway?

Hawkins' mother could tell her. Since her divorce she has become a regular at the Southpark Presbyterian Church where the preacher speaks of Jesus like he's a pretty nice guy. That preacher sniffed out her loneliness and has helped her find a path. He has shown Hawkins' mother how to set up the Sunday bulletin on the computer, has started her setting out the music for choir practice. Her name is Ruth, the preacher calls her Ruth.

Bjorn Toulouse is surprised when she meets her, expecting all mothers to be like her own, loud and spacey, keeping a kitchen where breakfast cereal crunched under your feet. But Hawkins' mother, with her blue eyes made huge and deep by her glasses, looks like a saint on a holy card. She stands up to meet Bjorn Toulouse and offers her small cold hand. Here is a woman who could starve herself to death for love.

Instead Ruth has waited. You can smell it in the room, like some small appliance left to run until its motor burns itself out. It's hard to understand what for. Ozone, Hawkins thinks, fat oxygen, a deeper blue.

Hawkins' old man sits in the armchair by the window. His skin is bleached out, the silver stubble brought out on his cheekbones by the sunlight. "You people," he says. He'd insult them if he could find words strong enough. Forty years ago he had run onto a beach under enemy fire without being wounded. Until now, that moment had sustained him. No mortgages, births of babies, assassinations, or impeachments of presidents could faze him. Hawkins wasted his time trying to tackle halfbacks.

"Call me Al," he tells Bjorn Toulouse. But she doesn't call him anything.

When Al used to knock softballs to Hawkins, the poor kid never could judge the path of their flights. Al didn't care. The satisfying squash they made going off the bat, like breaking a watermelon open by dropping it on a country road, took him back to a younger, stronger time. Hawkins, dumb as a retriever, would chase them down for hours.

"She shouldn't be here," Al says. Bjorn thinks he means her, but Ruth turns her head away as if she's been slapped. The old man's never slapped her, there was no need to. "Well then," Hawkins' mother says, fussing around with her purse and a library book.

"Your Mother's getting out of the kitchen."

This is how it always is, Hawkins thinks, actions don't make any sort of equal reaction. Everything happens out of proportion. Everything happens too fast.

"Your Mother couldn't stand the heat," his father told him when the divorce was going through. Hawkins' father always called her "Your Mother" whenever it was necessary to call her anything at all. Hawkins called his father "Sir." Yet Hawkins and his mother believe they were a happy family only lately gone to splinter.

Bjorn Toulouse has intercepted Ruth in the doorway. "Listen, we could talk or something," she tells her. Ruth offers her most gracious smile, one she has practiced many times to assure anybody who happens to catch an episode of Al's ugliness that her life is happy and placid in every respect. Bjorn Toulouse trails her down the hall and slips into the elevator behind her.

When she's inside and descending, Hawkins' mother allows herself to start her hyperventilated sobbing. It's all right, this is the one thing a hospital is good for. "OK, OK," Bjorn says, "get it all out," knowing that allowing for some small variations in syntax she's mouthing the words of her own mother to her on occasions as diverse as skinned elbows and stood-up dates.

"Who's your girlfriend?" Al says. "She looks like the kind who'd do it on the dining room table."

"I wouldn't know." It's true that one morning after both of them had gotten off the night shift Bjorn Toulouse offered Hawkins a bran muffin and one thing led to another. But she stopped it; his clumsy hands were stretching the elastic in her leotard with their groping. This was never going to work, she told him. It was months before they went back to bargain night at the Visualite together.

"Look at this," his old man says, standing up and shucking off his hospital issue PJs. You could make out the little pocket where his pacemaker was if you looked closely. But Hawkins sees the rounding belly over the limp prick, the empty balls, skinny thighs and shins barked how many hundreds of times in this lifetime, all knotted with blood vessels that seem much too close to the surface. Even the skin must wear thinner.

"You know what the Indians used to do," Al says while turning his pruney ass to Hawkins and pulling up his pajama bottoms, "throw the old ones out in the snow to die."

Hawkins has read the body replaces its cells every seven years. Who's to say that Al's replacements weren't defective? In their hometown, he sold life insurance. All he had to do was walk in the cafés and breakfast places and the stuff sold itself. Then those new cells came in and felt like busting loose so that he could no longer be another guy driving a Country Squire wagon. Now here's yet another bad batch. "Nobody's going to do that," Hawkins tells him.

"You should. You would if you loved me." Al climbs slowly onto the bed and stretches himself out, folds his arms over his chest, closes his eyes and frowns. "I'm ready."

Hawkins thinks he could tell Bjorn Toulouse it's not the wind at all but gravity that causes everything to break down: skin, organs, veins. The heart gets tired, pushing all that blood up to the head. Maybe it's natural to want to take it lying down.

Hawkins and his mother called Al's woman Elvira. When he came to campus on football Saturdays, Al would leave her waiting, fiddling with her mascara while parked in the fire lane in his white Riviera. Dark roots, a ring of makeup in the collar of her blouse, backless high-heel shoes, almost pretty and not so young, she used to have a better arrangement with a doctor or a lawyer. Like the Phantom in the funny papers, there's always an Elvira, silently changing from one woman to another while the natives try to act like everything is copacetic.

But there's no Elvira around here. Maybe Al's come to the last of the line, run out of love, if that's what it was.

"Getting any visitors?" Hawkins asks him.

"Your Mother has been sitting up here like a turkey vulture. They can smell death. Your Mother's blind as a goddamned bat, but she can smell. That's how she found me out."

"Didn't you want to get found out?"

Al groans and rises up in the bed and says, "I never wanted to hurt Your Mother. There's lots you don't know. She forced my hand." The blood is in his face now; he really could have a heart attack. He lets himself flop back down against the mattress and breathes in exaggerated desperation. "Get out of here. You've always been on her side." He begins pumping the call button for a nurse.

Hawkins must still obey him. When he's at the door, Al says, "You're getting plenty of pussy. Try going without it. You don't know a thing." The words push him out into the hall. Al hollers, "Get a decent job. Grow up, for Christ's sake."

Out on the street Ruth and Bjorn Toulouse wander through the stores that have sprouted up around the hospital. Ruth wonders at the changes wrought in the world while she hasn't been paying attention. One store sells only expensive stereo equipment, another oddly unattractive sandals. Others sell houseplants, knives and cutting boards, or bicycles. None have any customers, but the clerks don't seem to mind. They treat Bjorn Toulouse like someone they might remember vaguely from some party or concert. Of course, she is wearing a pair of the ugly sandals, as are some of the clerks they see. Others wear flip-flops.

"These stores seem so odd," Ruth says.

"I know, isn't it neat?" Bjorn Toulouse tells her. She hums a little tune and executes pirouettes around the stores, picking up the merchandise and handling it roughly before sitting it back in its place.

Ruth cannot decide what to make of this girl. She had smiled when she caught the name, but she regrets it. Maybe that's why the girl felt free to follow her into the elevator. Ruth decides Bjorn Toulouse has no manners. It's what the world has come to. At least Al knew better; his gaucheries were all designed to embarrass and offend her. And Hawkins is just clumsy. Ruth resents being caught out when she could control herself no longer.

Now they are in a bookstore with rocking chairs stuck around in every cranny and few books. A gray-haired man with a ponytail sits with his legs drawn under him and reads. When she passes, he looks up and smiles.

Bjorn Toulouse's round pink face looms into hers. "Listen to this," and she starts reading to her aloud. "Wholeness is health. Finding your own center can be hard when the emotional landscape keeps shifting. Peaks of happiness drop off to sloughs of despond. Somewhere out there is a peaceful plane, maybe even a plateau for you. Getting there can be the hard part. Guiding your emotional self like a Monopoly board piece (are you the worn-out shoe or the racing car?) over to this place can be too great a challenge. Just stop. Find your center before you strike out again . . ."

"Something to think about," Ruth says in a pleasantly noncommittal way when she realizes Bjorn has paused to get her reaction.

But she certainly hadn't intended for the girl to buy this book. Out in the street, Bjorn Toulouse presents it to her. Ruth smiles her gracious smile, and Bjorn leads her into a vegetarian restaurant for lunch.

"So," says Bjorn, "tell me all about Al."

Ruth looks at her and at the cover of her book, a mandala filled with many-armed gods and goddesses, and at her plate of rice with slabs of eggplant and yellow squash. She's tired and upset and won't be badgered any longer. She feels dizzy, but she says, "He thinks if he hurts me enough, I'll no longer love him." That wasn't what she'd intended to say at all, but saying it makes her feel better.

As he leaves his father's room, Hawkins manages to catch a nurse on her way to answer Al's frantic buzzing. "What's wrong with him?" he asks her.

"Who are you?"

"His son." .

The nurse gives him a long look like he's the parent of a kid running loose in a restaurant. "Can't get his prick up. That's just a guess." She smiles. "My professional assessment."

Hawkins looks down and sticks his hands in his pockets. "What can you do for that?"

"Well. . . ." They both hear Al's buzzer ringing down at the nurses' station. "I kind of like to slip into the room when the patient has dozed off, run my hand up under his gown, take his balls gently in my hand, and squeeze real hard. A little attitude adjuster." She smiles at him brightly.

Make this simple test: Which hurts more, having your nuts mashed or watching your life go to hell in a basket? Going down, Hawkins thinks maybe the hospital is the right place to conduct such a test, where the whiteness of the walls gives a person nothing to hang on to. Calcium would be that kind of chalky white. Bones. Hawkins has read that mice eat bones, and it's a good thing too. If they didn't we'd be walking around in a world piled thick with them.

When Hawkins finally finds Bjorn Toulouse and his mother, they are laughing and eating ice cream cones. "Where have you been?" he hollers at them. "I've looked all over the place for hours." He's exaggerating, but he has also gotten a parking ticket by now.

"Hawkins," Bjorn says, "is it true that when you were a baby you hid behind the refrigerator and wouldn't come out when you had company?"

He tells her no.

"Oh," Ruth says, "he was so cute when he was little, so shy. Only his father could get him to laugh. When they used to wrestle, he'd tickle."

"Tickling is cruel," Bjorn tells her. She doesn't know where, but she read that somewhere. Having met the old man, she's now convinced it's true.

Ruth cannot imagine why she would want rum raisin, the flavor of the rum tastes like medicine. If she could find a trash can, she'd throw the rest of her cone away. Instead, she offers it to Hawkins. Maybe it will calm him down; he's acting just like Al. And she wants him to drive her to her church so he can meet Gary Trice, her pastor. Ruth knows Hawkins will have an excuse, but she's already worked it out with Bjorn Toulouse. She'll drive Hawkins' Ford back to their complex so Hawkins can take Ruth.

Ruth's car is a tiny blue lozenge, almost new. In this way, Al still looks after her. He'll give her anything except what she wants the most. Hawkins climbs in, feeling like a gorilla in the undersized car. Alone with Ruth, he complains about wasting his day, about being tricked into this errand.

Bjorn Toulouse would be surprised to hear him bullying his mother. Hawkins is a man who stops to get turtles out of the highway when he sees them trying to make their slow way. But here, in the only corner of his universe where he has any special powers, he finds himself abusing them again. What kind of law of physics is he breaking now?

Never mind; Ruth is sure a talk with Gary Trice will turn her boy around, that they will clasp hands and slap each other on the back as soon as they meet. Gary was on the taxi squad for a season with the Atlanta Falcons. He has told Ruth about the damage to his joints, about the terrible scars on his knees and shoulders. He has told her that he cannot lift one of his arms above his head, a handicap that limits his range of ecclesiastical gestures.

There was a time when Hawkins would have been humbled and amazed to stand the presence of a former professional ballplayer, regardless of his capacity. In Ruth's mind, he remains stuck in that time: He wears a striped shirt and khaki slacks and poses jauntily leaning against the door of the family car. All he has to do is smile and his years of surly growls, his more recent years of absent stares simply fade away.

Pastor Gary sticks out a blackened paw to shake. In the other he holds an oddly shaped bottle. He's a large pillow of a man with shocks of yellow sticking out of his head and wire-rimmed glasses too small for his face. There's a smear of ink across the front of his knit shirt and more on his slacks. Behind him, a copying machine sits exposing its ugly secrets. "You know anything about these things?" Pastor Gary asks Hawkins.

It has something to do with the light putting an electrical charge against the piece of paper you're going to copy so that the ionized ink is pulled against the paper with different degrees of attraction. That's what Hawkins knows, but he doesn't know anything helpful such as how to fix one.

"Oh yeah?" says the preacher. Although he was never told this in divinity school, Pastor Gary has learned that helplessness often disarms a hostile soul. "Maybe you can figure out how to put this toner where it belongs."

The bottle slides smoothly into its place, surprising Hawkins. He's a terrible mechanic. What difference does it make when everything is wearing out anyhow? But he's pleased with himself now. As soon as he has all the pieces back in place, he's going to test the machine. While he's working, Hawkins can hear the preacher off somewhere washing up. He can't find anything to copy, so he sticks his hand under the rubber slab and pushes the button. Out pops a big white hand on a black field. Hawkins holds up his hand and examines it under the fluorescent lights of the Fellowship Hall. Once atoms fell like rain. Nobody stopped to wonder where they fell from, where they fell to. Nobody was even around except maybe God. Then an atom swerved. With God's connivance? Out of boredom? Regardless of the cause, the rest is history.

In some distant office he can hear his mother and Pastor Gary talking. What changes has Hawkins wrought? Molecules have been rearranged. From now on, everything will be different, won't it? He wipes his hand on his pants. The air in the Fellowship Hall is cool and stale like it hasn't been used much, like the air in a tomb. Above the large opening to the kitchen, there is a picture of Christ, the standard one of a deeply tanned man with gold highlights in his chestnut hair. Here's an answer, God's repairman. Except Hawkins sees nothing in the guy's expression to inspire confidence. Christ looks wistfully off into the sky. There's not a trace of knowledge or cunning about him. If he stopped for you broken down on the highway, you'd know that all he was going to do was offer you something to snack on while the tow truck came.

"So," Pastor Gary says, quite pleased. Is it because he's caught Hawkins staring at the picture of Jesus or because Hawkins has fixed the copying machine? "Your mother is just the sweetest soul. She's a blessing to me."

"Yeah," Hawkins says hoarsely. He should be nicer to this man; he means to be. He tries to imagine him sixty pounds lighter, full of rage and spleen, coming up out of his three-point stance to deliver a forearm shiver.

"Listen. . . ." Pastor Gary has closed his distance to within a foot of Hawkins. "Your mother tells me you're kind of at loose ends."

Hawkins doesn't say anything. He imagines himself as a rope unraveling.

"I went through a phase like that once." The trouble with preachers is all their crises take place without the aid of drugs or alcohol, in a well-lit coffee shop, and are solved by the time they eat a second jelly doughnut. So it was with Pastor Gary. Off the taxi squad one day, he found himself walking past the doors of Emory School of Theology the next. As soon as he entered those air-conditioned halls, he knew he had come home.

Ruth reappears after what she hopes is a decent interval, but Hawkins gives her a look that let's her know it was an overlong absence. Pastor Gary gives her a small shrug, his professional eye conveys a twinkle of regret. I must be lead, Hawkins thinks, heavy and dull. Cold.

"See if you can get this guy back here with you on Sunday." Ruth's smile is painful gratitude, despair. "No kidding. I'm really getting pumped up, it's going to be a good one."

On the way back to Hawkins' place, the car fills with argon, freon, something like that. Ruth looks out the side glass and hums a hymn. Hawkins knows it, "Almost Persuaded." He knows it from his childhood church where their preacher stood at the altar stiff as iron, challenging each and every soul to come forward and face its Maker. That was a preacher who came around to call during a Baltimore Colts game, confident his Maker would have little patience for the National Football League.

———————

This is not how it's supposed to be. We should live in shining aluminum cities covered with high glass domes, ride monorails to work or little wheel-less cars shaped like bullets. The ancients—either the Greeks or the Babylonians—foresaw all of this, only they imagined it was already here, a huge crystal ball surrounding our earth with the stars etched forever into its surface. How could they have guessed those very stars were out to betray us? Huge gassy balls sending licking flames out into space. Cosmic rays. And all of them burning out, falling in on themselves, becoming nothing, becoming worse than nothing. Nothing minus nothing.

"So how was the Big G?" Bjorn Toulouse asks. Hawkins knows she has been lurking behind her venetian blinds watching for his mom to leave. Now is not when you think. Now is Sunday. Hawkins has slipped through time and come out after church, a place he never planned to go.

"It was OK." He is taking off his sport coat with its epaulets of dust from hanging in the closet so long. He is taking off his tie, wide as a diving board.

"Come on, you were scared shitless."

He knows what she means, but it's not that way anymore. It seems like Jesus has worn himself out being angry, he's ready to be our buddy now. Pastor Gary packs them in, old and young, rich and middle class. The Youth wear shorts and sport shirts. There is always volleyball afterwards. Bjorn Toulouse says she thinks maybe it's better this way, but she is wrong. With Jesus out of the way, who does that leave to aim our guilt at?

For the first time Hawkins can feel the difference. The air in a church used to be thick and dense; he used to think he was going to need an iron lung to draw a mouthful. People pushed together on the pews got stuck to each other from all the excess molecules hanging around. Now everybody is shriveled and far apart, they wrap their arms around themselves to keep from floating away. He is sure there is less matter than there used to be.

Out in the complex parking lot Prentice wriggles like a snake out of the innards of his Kenworth cabover. Forty thousand dollars worth of matter, and it doesn't even run right. But Prentice will have to wait until he breaks it worse to call the shop wrecker to come get it. He has grown up too poor and too proud to think of anything else.

Guilt itself could be an element, a heavy one, still off the charts. Beyond uranium, beyond plutonium. Beyond berkelium and californium and all those other ones they hadn't thought up yet when Hawkins was in high school.

Catherine is out working on her tan beside the bean-shaped pool. She and Bjorn Toulouse have tea from time to time. She tells Bjorn that the strap marks from her suit are actually a help in her work, which is topless dancing.

"She's going to catch cancer," Hawkins says. He pictures a cosmic ray breaking into one of Catherine's skin cells, scattering her nucleus, mitochondria, and genetic material like a rack of pool balls.

It's the girl-next-door effect. Even though Catherine is up in the lights wearing a leopard skin G-string, each drooling guy knows she is just like the girl he can see sunning every day just over the fence. Prentice can't hold onto his tools for looking at her.

"Interchangeable parts," Bjorn Toulouse tells Hawkins, "alchemy." She knows it's not cancer but the bright lights and hard looks that tear Catherine down, tear anybody down, really.

The world will end on Sunday afternoon. Hawkins has known that since childhood. His old man sleeping with the paper like a pup tent on his lap—dreaming up a hard-on under there. His mother off in the house somewhere humming a reprise of the Hymn of Invitation. No ball game on TV, no way to escape. This is the family's day.

Sure enough, the world is slowing down to a wobble. Bjorn Toulouse can feel it too. "Let's find a stock car race we can go to." Ordinarily, Bjorn Toulouse disapproves of internal combustion; but today, when everybody's brain is already half full of carbon monoxide, what could it hurt?

But Hawkins says, "Let's go to the hospital to see the old man." Bjorn Toulouse has read about people like Hawkins in her self-help books. Throwbacks to the days when people went singing into flames to meet their God, went marching into enemy gunfire to serve their country. Watch out for this type, the books all tell her; they'll drown for love and take you choking with them.

"Didn't you ever wish you were an orphan? I did. I used to have this fantasy that both of them would get wiped out by a semi- when the air brakes failed."

"No," he tells her.

"They wouldn't feel a thing. Like bugs."

There are more bugs in the world than people, which shouldn't surprise you if you've ever tried wiping out just a small colony of them. Taken all together, they outweigh us. Millions could come and sit on us, and then what? A payback for thinking it's our world and we're the only ones in it.

Ruth will not be going along. Pastor Gary has told her it's OK not to for a while. "Let him stew in his own juice," he said. Hawkins was surprised; he didn't think Jesus left anybody to stew. Bjorn Toulouse says she has to whip up something with her lentils and dried tomatoes; Hawkins can try it when he gets back if he brings some imported beer.

Watching Hawkins drive off, Bjorn Toulouse thinks of a *Sons of Hercules* movie where another misunderstood guy with every impulse of love for his fellow person has been thrown into a cell by a dozen snarling Roman legionnaires. Lying there half-awake in nothing but his loin-cloth and muscles, he sees, or maybe only thinks he sees, the walls— the walls prickly with spikes like a cactus—starting to close in on him. They are. The walls are inching closer; the ceiling is dropping. Suddenly alert and reenergized, he's up, pushing his well-defined arms out against the walls, then up against the ceiling. Wait, Bjorn Toulouse would tell him, those spikes are only Styrofoam, that wall is just cardboard.

Still, she is thinking, as she watches Hawkins pull off with the corpse of a Sunday dragging behind him, he should go. For Ruth he has to go.

Hawkins could tell her Styrofoam is a first cousin to mustard gas. The leftover ingredients from that cardboard have already killed every fish in some sleepy mill-town river. Maybe those long chains of molecules, the kind Bjorn Toulouse is so crazy about, are the most untrustworthy kind.

Al is in his robe and sitting outside on a bench with a toothless old black man and a young white man. The white man wears a variety of tattoos and has recently had his head shaved. His pale blonde hair makes a downy fuzz on top. An egg making itself a chicken the hard way, Hawkins thinks. All three of them are smoking cigars while a nurse who looks familiar glowers at them from another bench across the skinny yard. "A patient's got his rights," Al says. The other two say, "Un hun."

"This is my boy," Al says, and instantly Hawkins feels himself shrunken, isolated. He stands scuff-footed on the sidewalk while the old man offers a thumbnail sketch of Hawkins' warehouse life and other recent disappointments. It makes no difference; even when Hawkins managed something worth bragging on, the old man fudged it up. A smarter, stronger, in every way more gifted Hawkins always existed out there somewhere for Al. He never knows what to think of the real one.

"Where's your squeeze?" the old man asks him, but Hawkins cannot make himself answer. "You ought to see her, one of those pale ones, you know? Looks like she hides under the refrigerator all day. Wears these dusty black clothes."

"Death," says the fuzzy head as he carefully rolls the ash off his cigar against the edge of their bench, "death and chaos, that's all there is."

"Want a cigar?" Al says, and Hawkins shakes his head. "Kid won't smoke. Smokes that marijuana, though." He waggles his cigar in Hawkins' direction. "You ought to see him then, all droopy eyed."

Hawkins sits down on the bench with the nurse, just on the edge, with barely enough of his ass against the wood to keep from falling off. He looks at a tattoo that seems to be a chicken or rooster standing on top of a globe. "Aren't death and chaos the same thing?" he asks the fuzzy one.

"Naw, man. Death is a real organized affair. Heaven or hell is the tough call, but after that, it's all one long drag."

Hawkins looks at the old black man to see what he is thinking. His arms are thick with heavy veins running along them like great rivers, his big hands rest on his knees. Maybe, Hawkins thinks, this guy works here. Maybe he is here for that second when his old man or fuzzy head jumps up and tries to run for the street.

"Because, I mean, in life anything can happen. I can transport my-self right out of here if I want to go—disassemble myself and put me back together somewhere else. It takes lots of energy, though, and they put drugs in your food here to keep your strength down. Don't you?" he says to the nurse.

"You're the one who's talking," she says, but she doesn't smile.

"Because this is what they don't want you to know: Chaos is good. Good for you, too."

Al beams his gaze on the old black man. "This guy once played ball with Satchel Paige." His voice is full of marvel. The man shifts shyly and smiles. In just such language Al has said, "an eight-point buck," "a four-pound bass," "a Pontiac Bonneville," and men got up and fol-lowed him out of the diner, down to his office where they insured their lives, their property, all they held sacred, with him.

You would think it would be easy to ride in the wake of such a man. A man whose friendly kibitzing at practice ought to get a boy a spot, if not in the backfield, at least at end.

Energy is finite. Around Hawkins, Al was a dark star, sucking every-thing in while he sat in front of the TV set, his kid hanging on his elbow ready to worship at the slightest invitation. It can't occur to Hawkins to blame Al. Acted on by gravity, electromagnetic fields, solar wind, ether wind, lunar attraction, who among us can claim to be truly responsible for anything that happens?

When Ruth calls that night, Hawkins will tell her that his old man is coming along fine. Which is the truth. Surrounded by a puddle of admirers who appreciate his free smokes enough to laugh at his stories, looking rich, handsome, and loved by a beautiful woman as surely as he is loved by all the orderlies who sneak him bourbon and keep the change, Al feels stronger already.

Hawkins is asleep when the space shuttle blows up. When he gets up in the middle of the afternoon and staggers out onto the balcony of his apartment, all he sees are the same fat pigeons clucking and pecking at the gravel, all he feels is too much heat coming off the fleet of worn-out cars below him. Across the way, Prentice sits in the bowels of his truck. When he sees Hawkins, he gets himself up and slowly walks toward him. At about fifty feet away, he hollers, "The rocket blew up," and looks somewhere above Hawkins' head as if he expects a piece to rain down right on their complex.

Hawkins does not understand. Prentice's voice is thick and slow; he must be doing Quaaludes again. "The rocket, the goddamned rocket."

They get in Hawkins' car and drive to a nearby sports bar. There a bartender and half a dozen shell-shocked customers watch as all fourteen color TV sets play and play again the picture of a white plume of smoke going haywire in a perfect blue sky. People, mostly men, come on the TV and babble. They don't know anything. Hawkins thinks of the schoolteacher. He sees her riding the rocket in her blue corduroy jumper and white turtleneck, her hair pulled efficiently behind her head, wearing one of those circular silver pins all the girls had when he was in high school.

"Up there talking to God," Prentice says. He is getting drunk. Hawkins considers doing the same. When you're drunk everything makes sense, everything is funny.

But Hawkins cannot get drunk, just as he knows he will not be able to sleep when he gets off work tomorrow morning. He thinks: Had he been awake, it all would have turned out differently. He remembers sitting in his fifth-grade classroom, a small black and white set on the teacher's desk, a ribbon of wire run up and clipped to the crate-like fluorescent fixture. All eyes stayed glued to the grainy image as the rocket began its shaky climb. He knew then it couldn't fall with every school child in American wishing it to rise. When this thing happened, Hawkins had been asleep.

In the future, people will comb the ocean floor looking for pieces of the rocket. They'll drag them back to Florida and try to put the whole thing together in a drafty hangar. Sublimation: when something goes straight from a solid to a gas.

"Are you still trying to date that Born To Lose woman?" Prentice asks him.

It's at the big end of the universe and at the little end where everything is fucked. In the solid middle, cars come and go, behaving themselves, obeying the law as laid down by Newton, as laid down by the Greeks. Molecules break apart, molecules come back together. If there is any molecular dust left over, nobody seems to notice. Why must Hawkins find himself stranded on the ends and not in the safe middle?

"Because I think she's all right." Prentice tells him. "She's getting me in touch with this guy who comes in the T-Bar and gives out those little religious cartoon books. You know, the ones where everybody goes through hellfire and is judged?"

It would drive out the impurities. It would come up behind you sitting on your custom-fitted reclining couch, all the dials in front of you suddenly going to zero, all the red lights coming on. You would know before you could name it. Before you could name it, you would be gone.

"Anyhow, she's going to get him to come by and take a look at my rig. They say he can fix things by laying on of hands."

"Right," Hawkins says. But he is thinking how even a schoolteacher's brain would be far from loaded to its carrying capacity until that moment when it would be filled up with understanding, then be a white hot cinder, then be nothing at all.

Pastor Gary likes to say grace even in a Chinese restaurant. They hold hands. Hawkins takes his mother's hand and Bjorn Toulouse's hand

and finds them feeling curiously like unusual laboratory specimens, oddly shaped hunks of flesh and bone. Grace is long and all-inclusive. Ethnic groups, politicians, countries Pastor Gary has never set foot in, all come up. The dead astronauts and their families are mentioned too, though by now Hawkins has heard some good jokes about them and feels less responsible.

Bjorn Toulouse tells Pastor Gary about the redneck preacher who has really fixed Prentice's Kenworth. Clogged injectors was all it was, but still he has pulled it off without as much as a pocketknife to help him. Bjorn has watched him, his face flush with concentration, as he wrapped his hands around the cold manifold and worked his mouth.

Pastor Gary, though, isn't impressed. He considers what's happened a stunt, a frivolity. But he wasn't there to see that engine fire and, after belching black for a while, settling down and idling smooth and clean. Prentice's wife wept. Prentice himself, after some prayerful moments with the healer in the cab, had come out to forswear booze and those CB gals who catch onto lonesome truckers driving with their ears on.

"Well," Ruth says, "God does work in mysterious ways." She has primed herself for mystery, would welcome some equivalent to the miracle of clean injectors in her own life. In this way, Pastor Gary can only disappoint her with his windy ponderings about why the lamb came from the thicket when it did.

Hawkins thinks about the ether wind, a wind that should be blowing all around us at gale force, but we wouldn't be able to feel it. He wishes it were out there; then everything could be explained.

Bjorn Toulouse snaps at Pastor Gary, "You don't know everything." She doesn't mean it; even though she has ordered Buddha's Delight, her head is muddied by a MSG buzz. "I mean, nobody knows everything. You have to believe some things are true even if you don't see them."

Pastor Gary says he believes in lots of things he can't see.

"Do you believe in heaven and hell?"

Pastor Gary says it all depends on what she means by heaven and hell. Maybe they are over-used concepts.

"Oh shit," says Bjorn Toulouse. "Some things you just know and don't have to figure out." This is exactly why she failed high school geometry. "Complex carbohydrates, get it?"

Pastor Gary shakes his heavy head. Yet here is a man who, in order to face his congregation of doctors, lawyers, and professors, must every Sunday put on a stained and faded game jersey underneath his vestments.

Ruth furiously chases a clot of rice around her plate with her fork. "What do you think, son?" she says to Hawkins.

Hawkins says, "I believe," then he says, "I think," then he gets quiet. He feels his ears burn, he decides maybe its the Szechwan dish. His mother and Bjorn Toulouse have gotten a hold on him and won't let go. "You know those Vietnamese monks who set themselves on fire during the war? I used to want to be one of them." Nobody else says anything.

You know those black holes everybody is talking about? What they are is so heavy with their own gravity—that is, if you believe in gravity anymore—that they bend their own light back onto themselves.

Hawkins' fortune reads, "You have ability, but lack self-confidence." Ruth thinks it reads like one of the many notes sent home from his teachers. Still, she is heartened. Knowing he would set himself on fire for something, whatever it might be, has heartened her.

Hawkins stands before the empty door of his father's room and finds it closed. He eases the handle, opens the door. A red-faced woman lies in his father's bed, her thick black hair fanned across the pillow. She wears a straitjacket, and heavy bands of webbing cross her body, anchoring her to the bed. Hawkins stares, having never seen a person so restrained before. The woman yanks her head until she manages to turn it partially toward him. "Scum," she says. "Lying bastard."

Hawkins closes the door. For some people there is always too much heat in the world. Rage dissipates as a gas and is too easily ignited. He makes his way to the nurses' station. "What happened to my father?"

It's the same nurse, she knows him. "Checked himself out. Checked out AMA."

"What's AMA?"

"Against medical advice."

"Is he well?"

She just smiles.

"I mean, is he OK?"

Another nurse answers him. "Some blonde babe came in here to get him. There he was sitting on his bed with his bag all packed like a kid ready to go off to his first summer camp. You know her? Glue-on fingernails about two inches long?"

A tight white skirt and a blouse that shows too much boob or too much back. Turning up when you have given up hope and expect only disaster, to clip the bad guys on the chin with her Skull Who Walks ring and pull off the rescue. "Elvira."

"Something like that. Maybe she knows that old ice cube trick," the first one says.

"What's that?" says Hawkins.

"Never mind. You're too young to be worrying about things like that."

From down the hall comes the woman's voice, much louder, "I'll kill you." The first nurse picks up a syringe and starts off.

"No kidding, honey. He's OK, no crazier than anybody else."

Air, fire, and water. If there really were just those three, and you really could keep a handle on them, you'd be all right. Fire. Hawkins knew it was a path to change, but what was to stop it from consuming the whole world?

Driving home down I-85, pressing to pass a semi- before he makes his exit, Hawkins blows a valve cover gasket. That's OK, it's happened before. He coasts along past the exit and under the overpass where he kills the lights and locks up. Then he walks up the exit ramp and down along a bright four-lane street into his empty warehouse of a city. He turns left on another, then onto smaller darker streets that will take him home.

The highway, the streets, all are lined with bits of glass smashed to diamonds. He sees them twinkle. Carbon. Not what you would think. It should be always black and sooty as coal. A dirty, friendly molecule, always wanting to stick to everything. It's in us all, in everything that matters. If Hawkins hurries he can get Bjorn Toulouse to drop him off at work.

Bjorn Toulouse has two vehicles, a VW bug and a Ducati motorcycle. "Let's take that," Hawkins always tells her.

"We can't." They can't because the bike, a leftover payback from a loan for a drug deal in the days when Bjorn Toulouse did those sorts of things, doesn't run and neither of them knows how to drive it anyway. So they get in the bug and drive. Bjorn Toulouse clings to the wheel at the ten o'clock and two o'clock positions, reads road signs, and obeys them. Velocity is a frightening thing; only by slow degrees has she conquered it.

At the light a low black car with blackened window glass pulls alongside them. Hawkins' eye begins to trace the predacious lines of the car, fish-like, shark-like down to its vestigial gill slits. The window glides down, smoothly, electrically. A woman with heavy dark hair and red lipstick looks at him across the narrow space. "Castanets," she says.

"Who was that?" says Bjorn Toulouse, who has never let her concentration slip from the light.

"Castanets."

"Uh-oh. You know what that means? It's a sign. A sign we should lay out of work."

"What would we do?" It's fifteen till twelve.

Bjorn shrugs. They could drive to Myrtle Beach. They could drive to the Blue Ridge Parkway. They could go to an all-night truck stop that wasn't the T-Bar and eat pancakes. They go to the late show at the Visualite.

It's a tedious foreign movie about clowns. People seem to do nothing but get in front of the camera and talk. When, Hawkins wonders, will they get to the clowning? But it turns out that European clowns aren't so funny after all. Maybe because they've been at it longer.

A clown stands on the packed dirt floor of a circus tent. He plays a mournful solo on a trumpet. Far off, he thinks he hears it echoed. He cocks his ear, he plays again. The echo sounds a little louder. He tries once more, he walks a little way, then again. Finally, he finds his buddy, the other clown, high in the empty grandstands. Hawkins is taken by surprise by this touching moment. Bjorn Toulouse puts her head lightly on his shoulder and does not move it as they sit through the credits.

There's nothing here but neutrons, electrons, pi-mesons, and quarks. Somehow they hold the world together. They've held it together so far anyway. Hawkins tries to relax his grip on the armrest.

The unfamiliar names roll by to happier circus music. A tuba starts burping and belching a beat, then a bassoon picks it up and plays a sneaky little melody. A clarinet flies up over them both and a trombone says something more sinister. Steadily, the tempo increases. Hawkins feels like this music wants him to go somewhere, to get up and follow it. Bjorn Toulouse is skipping him out of the theater.

Outside, the air is light and fragrant. The diesel smell of the city seems to have gone away somewhere. Things seem different. Hawkins imagines his father's white Riviera beating westward: Nashville, Las Vegas, L.A. His bank account is cleaned out, and Elvira curls beside him on the seat. Hawkins pictures his mother sorting sheet music in the Fellowship Hall. She hums "Holy, Holy, Holy" to the whir of the nearby Xerox machine. Just beyond, the sanctuary is dark, but soon enough its windows will be illuminated. Ruth expects the miracle light might bring.

Now, Bjorn Toulouse is telling him, is the time for a big stack of pancakes. After that, who knows? Hawkins decides things really are different, but in what way? Maybe it's just a molecular realignment, a swerve.

When he drops off to sleep near morning, Hawkins has a dream. In it he and Bjorn Toulouse are riding her Ducati to the Outer Banks. He has been there once in his Ford, back when he had faith in it. Although he has never been on a motorcycle in his life, he is driving, letting the bike pull them down deep into the curves, riding them up straight and clean as an arrow down impossibly long straight stretches. Without looking at the speedometer, Hawkins knows they are going a hundred, then a hundred and twenty. He feels no fear, trusting to physics to make a way through the world for them. The air is sharp and stings their faces, but they are not cold, the light is indigo above them, then azure, then a flaming orange near the horizon where the sun will come up any minute. The smell of salt, the taste of salt surround them. Surely the ocean must be near. They sweep along the long rising bridge that takes them off the mainland.

Now they are parked along the road and walking up and over the dunes to the sea. Though he knows they were riding bareheaded— his ears still sting and burn—they now carry helmets under their arms like athletes or astronauts and wear sleek silver outfits. He discovers he has grown incredibly handsome, but he is still Hawkins. He sees she is beautiful, but still Bjorn Toulouse. Now they are naked and standing in the gentle surf; the tide is ebbing around their feet. New muscles in his chest and arms ripple as he walks into the ocean. Where is he going? Bjorn Toulouse is wondering, and he knows this even though she hasn't moved her mouth to speak. "To be with the dolphins," he answers.

"Oh shit," she tells him. But as he strikes out swimming, he knows she is coming too.

Frank Soos is a professor of English at the University of Alaska in Fairbanks. He is also the author of *Early Yet*, a collection of short stories forthcoming from Saint Andrews College Press in 1998, and *Bamboo Fly Rod Suite*, a collection of essays forthcoming from Georgia in 1999.

The Flannery O'Connor Award for Short Fiction

David Walton, *Evening Out*

Leigh Allison Wilson, *From the Bottom Up*

Sandra Thompson, *Close-Ups*

Susan Neville, *The Invention of Flight*

Mary Hood, *How Far She Went*

François Camoin, *Why Men Are Afraid of Women*

Molly Giles, *Rough Translations*

Daniel Curley, *Living with Snakes*

Peter Meinke, *The Piano Tuner*

Tony Ardizzone, *The Evening News*

Salvatore La Puma, *The Boys of Bensonhurst*

Melissa Pritchard, *Spirit Seizures*

Philip F. Deaver, *Silent Retreats*

Gail Galloway Adams, *The Purchase of Order*

Carole L. Glickfeld, *Useful Gifts*

Antonya Nelson, *The Expendables*

Nancy Zafris, *The People I Know*

Debra Monroe, *The Source of Trouble*

Robert H. Abel, *Ghost Traps*

T. M. McNally, *Low Flying Aircraft*

Alfred DePew, *The Melancholy of Departure*

Dennis Hathaway, *The Consequences of Desire*

Rita Ciresi, *Mother Rocket*

Dianne Nelson, *A Brief History of Male Nudes in America*

Christopher McIlroy, *All My Relations*

Alyce Miller, *The Nature of Longing*

Carol Lee Lorenzo, *Nervous Dancer*

C. M. Mayo, *Sky Over El Nido*

Wendy Brenner, *Large Animals in Everyday Life*

Paul Rawlins, *No Lie Like Love*

Harvey Grossinger, *The Quarry*

Ha Jin, *Under the Red Flag*

Andy Plattner, *Winter Money*

Frank Soos, *Unified Field Theory*